Carolyn Alexander

The
Settlement

Carolyn Alexander

The Settlement

Introductory

The Settlement is red-hot erotic, steamy, alluring, and climactic. If you like seductive thriller romances that leave on the edge of your seat, then turn the pages to see these riveting chain of events unfold, as we conclude the sequel to The Arrangement.

Over a year has passed when sexy Lorna Collins comes face to face with the unforgettable Phillip Powell, the man that shook her world apart. Soon realizing that their love was more than a summer romance, they break all boundaries and arrangements, to be together.

When Theodore Powell learns that Phillip and Lorna have reconciled, a love that was forbidden, his burning anger becomes out of control. He will stop at nothing to eliminate Lorna from his son's life.

Secrets and lies are revealed leaving Phillip outraged, wanting his father to pay. The two of them head back home to Yale, Michigan with a vengeance that leaves Lorna's life hanging in the balance. Phillip finds himself in unfamiliar territory with the death of a loved one.

How will Phillip settle the score with compassion or an eye for an eye?

The Settlement

A NOVEL

Suspense Thriller Fiction

Part 2 of The Arrangement

<u>Acknowledgement</u>

A huge thanks to:

My husband Brian, for believing in my dreams. My two children, Michelle and Nicholas, for giving me that push I needed and always believing my dreams could become a reality. My two sisters, Diane and Colleen, and brother Joe, for your words of encouragement, advice, and love. Also, my brother Mark that went on to be with Our Lord Jesus Christ. Mark was my true inspiration for writing, and I wish he were still here to see that I finally did it.

My editor and friend, Teresa Frazer Gravlin, whom I've known for many years. You have truly been a Godsend to me. I'm so grateful God crossed our paths all those years ago. Thank you, Teresa, for all your hard work and for making my books the best they could be.

Most of all, I thank God every day for all the Wisdom and Knowledge He has given me to write books. Without the Lord Jesus Christ in my life, I'd be nothing and have nothing. All Glory goes to our Heavenly Father above!

Special Thanks

I want to thank my two very dear friends, John, and Michelle Hamilton, for allowing me to sit in their store while I wrote The Arrangement, then The Settlement. It was truly inspirational being surrounded by all those beautiful antiques.

I love you both dearly, and thank you!

Trash to Treasures
8008 Lakeshore Rd, Lexington, Mi. 48450

Books by CAROLYN ALEXANDER

Three Doors Down

The Arrangement

The Settlement

Carolyn Alexander

The Settlement

The Settlement

Chapter 1

Lorna collected her composure, turned on a dime, and started to run as fast as she could, as she heard Phillip calling her name in the distance. Feeling her heartbeat in her throat, she finally made it to her dorm room, breathless, fumbling with her keys at the door. She then nervously placed the key in the keyhole, fumbling for the handle. She opened the door and quickly stepped inside, immediately closing the door behind her. She began walking around in circles pacing back and forth across the floor, muttering under her breath, "Oh my gosh, Phillip! Phillip! On my first day here. Oh, my goodness, he looks good. Now he knows I'm here... now what? Now what, Lorna? What are you going to do now?" Her legs were still shaky and weak and her mind was spinning trying to come up with an answer to her problem.

She began asking herself out loud, "If I did talk to Phillip again, where would I start? What would I say first? You're an asshole! Or would I be nice? Would I ask him why he used me as a pawn in this twisted little game he was playing with his crazy rapist father? Would I ask him why he never came back home to me, even after his father told him I was pregnant with his baby?

Would I ask him where he was when I buried our daughter? Why Phillip? Why didn't you come back home? Or would I tell him how much I've loved him and missed him and that I forgive him? But, I don't forgive him! He used me and hurt me...bottom line!", she whispered with an angry look on her face as tears fell down her cheeks.

Not only did Lorna see Phillip for the first time in over a year, she realized she was still in love with him. Lorna sat down on her bed, buried her face in her hands and cried. Her heart was so broken. She had so many unanswered questions, but she knew even though she and Phillip were now in the same place together, she still couldn't talk to him because Theodore Powell had her watched to make sure she didn't speak to Phillip.

The door to her room suddenly flew open. A girl with curly blonde hair and glasses came slamming through the doorway with her arms full of stuff and her parent's right behind her. She stopped, Lorna looked up, and the girl walked over and held out her hand. "Hello, I'm Connie Davis. I'm from Canton, Michigan. Where are you from?"

Lorna stood up, wiped the tears from her face and said with a wry smile, "Hi...I'm Lorna Collins. I'm from Yale, Michigan."

Connie, with a concerned look on her face, asked, "are you ok?"

"Yes, just a rough day. I'll be okay...thank you for asking."

As Connie got settled in, the girls talked a little, but Connie did most of the talking. They went to bed, but Lorna laid awake most of the night thinking about Phillip. The next morning, the girls got up, got themselves ready, and spent the whole day getting to know each other while walking around on campus and talking to other students. They both settled right into what would be their home for the next four years of undergraduate classes together. Connie was also studying to be a pediatrician. They had a few classes together, which was nice.

Now, two weeks post-Phillip, Lorna found herself hiding and peeking around every corner as she walked around campus. She was so afraid she would run into Phillip. She had gone over a hundred scenarios in her head of what she would do or say and, secretly, deep in her heart, hoped she would run into him. Lorna so desperately wanted to see Phillip again, but there were no sightings at all, which was Phillip's typical "method of operation." It was not a surprise that he would disappear, which made her wonder even more what happened.

Classes were starting on the following Monday and Lorna was so excited to get started, she was more than ready. The thought of putting all the past bullshit behind her and moving on to a brand new life gave her chills. Lorna and Connie were becoming good friends, but there was something Lorna did not reveal. She didn't tell her new friend about Phillip or the fact that she'd had a baby...a baby she had to bury.

That Friday and Saturday held nothing but big parties hosted by the fraternities recruiting new members. Everyone was signing up to be part of some kind of fraternity and Lorna wanted nothing to do with it. All she wanted to do was get her education and move on. Connie, on the other hand, wanted more out of her college experience than that. Connie wanted to be a sorority sister with whoever would accept her. Lorna felt that she was just looking for someone to love her and be accepted, somewhere to make her feel alive. Connie was never accepted into any sorority, but she attended enough frat parties to fill her social calendar from the first day of school until Thanksgiving break. From what Lorna heard, Connie was the life of the party, and she was always trying to get Lorna to go to with her.

Monday morning at 5:00 a.m. Lorna's alarm went off and she jumped right out of bed, eager to get to class and get her new life underway. She grabbed her towel, all her bathroom supplies, and headed down the hall to the bathroom. There were two other girls in there getting ready. They both smiled at Lorna and politely said hello to her. Lorna reciprocated with a broad smile on her face, "Good morning."

She took a quick shower and got dressed in a black pleated skirt with a white blouse and a black scarf around her neck. She towel-dried her hair and pulled each side up with bobby-pins, brushed her teeth and put on red lipstick, and was ready to go. She walked back into the dorm room and noticed

Connie was still sleeping. Lorna reached down, nudged her shoulder and said in a loud tone,

"Connie, you better get up--you're going to be late for the first day."

Connie made some noises then pulled her pillow out from under her head, covered her face with it and in a muffled voice asked what time it was. Lorna told her it was almost 6:00 a.m. and that she only had an hour to get ready. Connie quickly pulled the pillow off her head, whipping it against the wall by her bed. She tossed the covers off of her and slowly sat up on the edge of her bed. Sitting there for a minute, she rested her face in her hands and then ran her hands through her hair. She stood up, collected her stuff and left for the bathroom.

Lorna thumbed through her syllabus and books while she patiently waited for Connie to return. She set her things down, let out a sigh and stood up. She was getting nervous and anxious, worried that Connie was going to make them late. Just as she had that thought, Connie came through the door much more alive than when she left. She was wearing a cute powder blue dress with light-yellow buttons and a white sweater. Her curly blonde hair was up in a ponytail and she wore red lipstick and cat-eye style glasses. She was a very pretty girl, Lorna thought to herself. They grabbed their things and headed out the door--off to the beginning of their new life.

Lorna's first class was Physiology. She and Connie didn't share a class until 1:00 p.m., Human Anatomy. They parted ways, each going in their different directions. Lorna had butterflies in her stomach as she walked with the rest of the students into a large room which looked like a theater. Everyone marched single-file to their seats and sat down. Lorna got adjusted in her chair, pulled out her books, paper, and pencil; she was ready. The room now filled with a soft buzz and some laughter. Then, a side door opened near the front of the class and in walked the professor. He laid his briefcase down on the desk and walked over to blackboard. Reaching down, he picked up a piece of chalk and wrote, Professor Johnson, Physiology 101. He turned around saying,
"Welcome everyone! Please take out your required books and syllabus for my class." Lorna almost threw up.

Professor Johnson, in his late thirties, stood at the front of the class wearing a double-breasted brown tweed suit. He had dark brown hair, a mustache and beard. He smoked a pipe and had eyes of steel. Although Professor Johnson was a younger version, he looked so much like Theodore Powell that they could have been twins. Lorna felt like her entire insides flipped. He started to talk, and Lorna completely zoned out. She drifted off, remembering Theodore coming out of Lois' room adjusting his pants. Someone laughed in the class and Lorna snapped back to reality and started listening to the professor. He went over the syllabus and what he expected out of them for the term. Lorna took a lot of notes and the class read from their books. They were given their homework assignment.

After class, Lorna was getting hungry, so she went to the cafeteria to get something to eat. When she walked into the cafeteria and went to the counter, she noticed two older ladies were behind the counter wearing hair nets and white uniforms. One of the ladies asked, with a raspy voice,

"What can I get for you?"

"I'll take a cup of black coffee and toast." A few minutes later the lady came back.

"There you go," she said, sliding the tray onto the counter.

Lorna slid her tray down to the cash register at the end of the counter. The lady at the cash register, in her 50's, had dark-red hair and looked like she'd had a rough life. She looked up at Lorna, smiled, and rang up her order.

"That will be 50 cents, Hun." Lorna reached out, handed her a dollar, and the lady handed her back 50 cents.

"Thank you. Have a nice day."

"Thank you. You too," Lorna said, smiling back at her.

Lorna took her tray and made her way to the seating area, where she found a table by the window. She sat down, closed her eyes, thanked the dear Lord for her food and the blessing of being able to attend The University of Michigan and said "Amen." Opening her eyes, she looked out the window and there was Phillip standing by a tree talking and laughing with some other guys.

Phillip, she thought. There you are. Where have you been? She sat quietly eating her toast, drinking her coffee, and watching the love of her life, right outside the window.

The Settlement

Chapter 2

Lorna's next class was Chemistry. Her enthusiasm was still high. She loved every bit of her new experience, much more than she'd ever imagined. Although seeing Phillip in between classes rattled her a little, Lorna went on with her daily routine as though she didn't see him. She'd decided she wasn't going to let Phillip's presence ruin her day or alter her experience at college, something she'd been waiting for her whole life.

Lorna made her way across campus to her Chemistry class. This class was different; it was a lab. Everyone walked in and took a seat around a table. The side door opened and in walked a salt-and- pepper-haired firecracker of a woman. She was in her late fifties with glasses dangling from a chain she had hung around her neck and was no bigger than a pound of soap.

She, too, went straight to the chalkboard and wrote Professor Dempsey, Chemistry.

Turning around, Mrs. Dempsey said in a very soft, sophisticated voice, "Good Morning class, welcome to Chemistry. Here, we'll have a lot of fun! If you could please take out your syllabus and your book for this class, I'm going to take roll call. Please say 'here' when I say your name."

Lorna got out her syllabus and book. The Professor slid her glasses onto her tiny-framed face, then proceeded with roll call. Name after name was called, then she heard "Lorna Collins." Lorna answered, "Here." After a few more names, she heard the Professor say, "Phillip Powell," and a voice from the back echoed to the front with "here." Lorna snapped her head around and looked in the direction of the voice.

There he sat at the back of the room looking as gorgeous as ever. Lorna's heart fell to her stomach. She couldn't believe Phillip was in one of her classes. Lorna quickly looked back once more and he was staring right at her. Her throat got thick and she could barely breathe. Her hands began to shake. Holy shit! Now what! What am I going to do about this one? Lorna thought why is Phillip in my chemistry class? He's a second-year medical student?

The Professor talked, made a few jokes, and they went over what they'd be doing in her class. She asked questions to get to know everyone, then she let everyone out early. Professor Dempsey told the class that within the next couple of weeks she'd be pairing everyone off into groups with four people in each group. She told everyone to have a fantastic day and that she'd see them on Wednesday.

Lorna bent down to pick up her books and stuff off the floor and stood up, tossing her long blond hair out of her face. Just as she did, Phillip was walking up toward the class looking right at her. He didn't blink or smile, just looked her up and down with his big green eyes. He arched an eyebrow at her and walked by with his books in one hand and the other in the pocket of his cuffed jeans and his hair greasy in a duck-butt. Lorna's heart broke. Phillip looked at her like she was a stranger. Lorna thought to herself that this would be an exciting few months spent together.

Walking out of class with her books held against her chest and a downcast face, Lorna shuffled down the hall to meet Connie. Stepping outside, she noticed Phillip standing with a bunch of people by the sidewalk talking to a girl. With her heart beating fast, palms sweating and legs shaky, Lorna moved quickly past them. She never looked up to even let Phillip know she saw him there.

Lorna made her way to the other side of campus in record time. Connie was walking right toward her. They both smiled at each other, then they both went to the cafeteria to get lunch. Lorna got an egg salad sandwich, chips, and water. Connie got a cheeseburger, fries, and Coke. They paid for their food and took their trays to a table in the back.

Almost everyone they passed said hello to Connie. Connie was funny. She had a pleasant personality, so upbeat and bubbly, and she always made Lorna laugh. Everyone was starting to know and like her.

They sat there discussing their classes, their professors, and laughing together. They were excited to go to anatomy class together. Connie devoured her cheeseburger like she hadn't eaten in a week. Lorna dropped her head and gave thanks to God for her food. Connie started to say something to Lorna and noticed she was praying.

When Lorna was finished, Connie said to her, "What was that? Do you always pray?"

Lorna said, "Yes, you should always thank God for the food He provided for you."

With a chuckle, Connie said, "God didn't give me this food, my parents did!"

"That's where you're wrong. Everything good comes from the God above. Don't you pray?"

"No, I don't know how," Connie said, stuffing her fries in her mouth.

Lorna asked if she believed in the Lord and Connie told her that she wasn't sure. She knew there was something out there bigger than her, she just wasn't sure what "it" was. Lorna explained that she could teach her about God and how Jesus Christ died on the Cross for us.

All of a sudden, Connie, with burger hanging out of her mouth, said, "Holy shit balls! Who is that?"

Lorna looked up, "Who?"

"Him! Him over there!" She pointed with her bony finger in the direction of Phillip, who was walking up to the counter to order something to eat. Connie was so excited she couldn't keep her eyes off of him. With a look of eagerness on her face, Connie said, "I've got to know who that is! Isn't he dreamy?"

Lorna looked at him and thought to herself, yes, absolutely. I've always thought so, but looked over at Connie and said, "I suppose so. He's not my type."

Connie looked at her with a surprised look on her face. "What? How can you not think he's gorgeous?"

"I didn't say that. Yes, he's very good looking, but he's not my type. I guess everyone has different taste," Lorna stated as she dropped her head.

Connie jumped up and told Lorna she'd be right back.

"What? Where are you going?"

"I'm going to introduce myself to that dreamy guy," she quipped as she wiped the food off her face and clothes.

"What... no your not!" Lorna said to her in a voice that even she didn't recognize, sounding like a mother bear protecting her cubs.

"Dang, Mom, cool it! I'll be right back." Connie opened her lips wide, showing her big white teeth, and said, "Do I have food in my teeth?"

Lorna let out a chuckle, looked at her teeth, and said, "No." Connie started walking away in a near run. Lorna kept whispering for Connie to come back to the table but she kept right on going in the direction of Phillip. Lorna drew her eyes to Phillip, who was standing there all alone, looking so vulnerable and sad. She watched Connie get closer to him. All of a sudden, she couldn't breathe. She was astounded and in panic mode. Lorna grabbed her stuff, threw her food in the trash, and tossed the tray on the ledge. She bolted for the doors, pushing them open with her hands, and made her way through a smoke-filled hall. Her eyes were drawn to the bench in front of her. She quickly sat down to get her bearings again. Connie came outside looking for her about 2 minutes later.

She looked at Lorna and said, "What the hell? What was that all about?"

Lorna thought real quick, then said, "Oh sorry, I felt sick all of a sudden and needed some air."

"Well, Mr. Gorgeous in there is taking me out this Friday," whirling her hands in the air.

Lorna gasped as she listened to the news that Connie delivered to her about Phillip and she almost started to cry.

"No, I'm kidding. I wish, though. His name is Phillip. He said he has a girlfriend," Connie said with sheer disappointment on her face.

"Did he say with who?" she asked Connie with wide eyes.

Connie looked puzzled, then pushed her glasses up on her nose and said, "No, he didn't, but I didn't think you cared?"

"I don't. I was just wondering. I thought maybe we might have seen Phillip's girlfriend before."

"Well, I don't know who it is," Connie stated, "but I didn't figure a guy like that would be single." Her voice trailing off, she told Lorna, "What I could do with a guy like that!"

Lorna said, "We better get going." They walked together to their anatomy class. Reaching the class with a few minutes to spare, they started mingling with a bunch of other kids. Well, Connie was mingling and Lorna was just a shadow in the crowd. They all took their seats. Connie and Lorna sat next to each other. Lorna noticed a few of the guys made it a point to sit by Connie. This class, too, was set up much like a lab, only without the chemistry bottles. Instead, this one had a fake skeleton hanging on a hook in the corner with lots of jars of human parts in formaldehyde. There were sterile instruments on trays and microscopes and big, bright lights hanging over the tables in the back.

Unlike the other classes Lorna had been to, the professor walked in the same door they did. He was young and handsome. He walked to the front of the class, wrote his name on the blackboard, Professor Donovitz, Anatomy, then turned to face everyone. Connie leaned in and whispered to Lorna that she would love to see his anatomy and then laughed. Lorna smiled and thought that her new friend was crazy, but she was right, he was adorable.

Professor Donovitz was in his early thirties, blonde haired, and had blue eyes with the start of crow's feet in the corners. He had a beautiful smile, perfect teeth, and a nice trim body that you could see threw his shirt, revealing his six-pack. He had a gold band around the ring finger of his left hand. He told the class proudly that he was married with a little girl at home. Lorna thought it was going to be challenging to stay focused with a teacher that good looking. She quickly scanned the room, making sure there were no more surprise visits from Phillip. All clear, she thought, and then put her focus back on the main attraction.

Lorna took lots of notes while the professor talked. Connie was too busy giggling with her new found boy-toys.

Professor Donovitz said, "You're about to understand the human body and all its mechanics. You'll get to know each bone of the human body, how it works and why. In this class, we will dissect all kinds of things, learn some interesting things together, and have fun. One thing you should know about me, though, is that I give pop quizzes a lot to make sure you're paying attention in my class. So, Class, think about who you might want to be lab partners with and next week that's who you'll spend the term with." He dismissed the class. Filing out, everyone started walking back to their dorm rooms.

Connie said, "Hey, a bunch of us are going to the pub off campus. Do you want to come with us?"

"No, but thank you though. I have homework to do," Lorna said as a flash of concern flickered over her face.

"C'mon. It's going to be fun," Connie said with excitement.

"No. I appreciate the offer, but I have to do my homework. Don't you have any?"

"Yes, Mom. I'll do it in the morning. Our first class doesn't start until 10 a.m. I'll have lots of time."

"Okay, if you say so," Lorna said with doubt in her voice.

The girls had Medical Terminology together, and Lorna knew if she went out with Connie she'd never be ready for that class. Connie left with two of the guys that were in their anatomy class.

Connie came back with a bang when she opened the door. It was so hard and fast, it slammed into the dresser behind the door. Lorna was so startled she almost jumped out of bed. Connie was loud and drunk, laughing and singing with no respect for her roommate sleeping. Lorna got up and turned the light on, telling Connie to be quiet.

"Lorna! Lorna, you should've come with me tonight. We had so much fun," she said, as she slurred her words and the room instantly smelled of alcohol.

"Connie, you need to get to bed. We've got class in the morning." Lorna walked over to Connie to try and help her get into bed.

"Shhh! Don't worry. I'll be ready." Sitting down on the edge of her bed, she then laid down, and popped up just as quickly with her hand over her mouth as she ran for the door. She quickly opened the door and bolted for the bathroom. Lorna knew she was going to throw up. A few minutes later, Connie came back to the room, took half her clothes off and laid on the bed. Lorna went back to bed, curled under the covers, and looked at her alarm clock. It was 2:43 in the morning! She was angry that Connie went out and got drunk with those guys, came home so late, and now she was sick. She fluffed her pillow under her head aggressively, let out a big sigh, then rolled over toward the wall. Connie had gotten up two more times in the course of the night to puke. Lorna's alarm went off at 7 a.m. As she rolled over to turn it off, she noticed Connie sleeping on the floor.

Lorna was so tired she felt like she'd been out all night drinking with Connie. Lorna got up, grabbed her stuff and headed to the shower. When she returned to the room, Connie hadn't moved a muscle. Lorna leaned down and moved Connie but she didn't budge. Lorna tried several times to get Connie off the floor to get ready for class.

It was now 9 o'clock and even yet, Connie wasn't up or ready. She had her homework to do from the day before and she was still sleeping. Lorna got her stuff together, then left without Connie. Lorna decided to get some coffee and toast before class to help wake her up. She made it to her medical terminology class and yawned almost the entire time.

The class ended, and Connie never showed up for her first day. Lorna was so angry about last night that it was burning her up inside.

When class dismissed, she went back to her dorm since she didn't have another class until 1o'clock. When she returned to the dorm, Connie was still sleeping on the floor in the same position. She slammed the door shut. Connie rolled over, then looked up.

With a raspy voice, Lorna heard Connie ask what time it was. When Lorna told her it was 11:45 a.m., Connie jumped up off the floor. Swaying back in forth, she held onto her head, letting out a loud "FUCK!" White as a ghost, she told Lorna she needed to sit down.

"Are you ok?" Lorna asked. Even though she was still mad at her, Lorna was concerned about her.

Connie laid back on her bed saying, "Holy shit, I feel like a truck hit me. Why didn't you wake me up for class?"

Lorna pushed her eyebrows together as anger built up inside of her again. She said, "I tried. You wouldn't budge so I left without you. I wasn't missing the first day of class."

Connie looked over at her and said, "But it was ok if I didn't go, right?"

Lorna got up, grabbed her books for her biology class, then headed toward the door.

Connie said, "What? You're leaving?"

"Yes, I'm leaving. I have my biology class at 1 o'clock," Lorna told her with a snarky tone.

"Well, will you let me use your notes from our terminology class today?"

Lorna stood there thinking about it, biting her bottom lip, and then said, "Yeah, I guess." She went out and slammed the door behind her, so mad at Connie her blood was boiling. Mumbling under her breath to herself, "Just because she doesn't care about her education doesn't mean I have to throw mine all away too."

Lorna made it to her class with time to spare. She stood outside leaning against the wall with her head down pondering the situation with Connie but, all the while, her thoughts kept going back to what Connie told her about Phillip having a girlfriend. Her thoughts then went back to Connie and she told herself she had to let it go. It was not her problem or her life. Phillip made his bed and now he can lay in it. Connie was a big girl. She could do whatever she wanted, and to hell with Phillip! He had his chance and blew it. By the time class was dismissed and Lorna made it back to her dorm, Connie was gone.

As she entered the room, she saw her bed unmade, clothes thrown all over, and the whole room smelled like puke. She flung the door open to air it out. As Lorna's anger flared again, she wondered if Connie was going to come in late and wake her up again. Sure enough, she did, and almost every night after. Connie was missing class all the time. When she did finally show up and grace everyone with her presence, she would fall asleep in class. She was starting to look rough and losing weight. Lorna was beginning to get concerned about her behavior. Lorna thought she had to be failing her classes, she was hardly in class. She never did homework or studied, and always wanted to borrow notes.

Connie was on a fast track to a road of destruction and Lorna had no idea how to help her friend. Nothing she said or did got through to Connie. She was wild and out of control. Lorna knew she had to help her before she flunked out of school or worse.

The Settlement

Chapter 3

The days and weeks were clicking along fast.
Lorna was getting into a solid routine of school,
homework and the disruptions of Connie in the
middle of the night, which were more often than
not. Lorna tried to talk to Connie on several
occasions, but Connie didn't care to hear it. Lorna
was almost sure that Connie was doing something
more than drinking. She acted high even when she
wasn't drinking and Lorna was genuinely worried
about her. She also considered talking to someone
about it, but who?

That Wednesday, Lorna went to Chemistry class.
After doing roll call as usual, the Professor said,
"Today, class, we're going to break into groups of
four, then we're going to start a project that will be
30% of your final grade. When you hear your

names, please get up and move to your group."
Name after name she yelled out and then she heard,
"Phillip, Scott, Tammy, and Lorna, please join each
other at a table." The whole room was a shuffle of
musical chairs. When everyone was seated and
settled in, Lorna was sitting right next to Phillip.

Phillip looked at Lorna with a wry smile, revealing
part of his perfect charm. With his incredibly
handsome, sculptured face and manly, chiseled chin
he didn't say a word. Lorna wanted to reach over
and touch him so bad. She could smell him; it was
so familiar that it was intoxicating. He is so
handsome, she thought. Even after all this time and
what he'd done to her, she still wanted him. He had
a girlfriend now and he belonged to some other girl.
How could this be? Phillip was mine and we had a
baby together! A baby, of course, that he didn't
want. Hand's off, Lorna, she reminded herself.

The Professor had laid out the project that was in
front of them for the next six weeks. She explained
that most people think that because chemistry is
seen as a rigorous A level that everyone expected
them to approach it rationally. Although these
attributes are valued, she didn't want them to do
that. The Professor wanted them to come up with
something unique, thinking outside of the box if
you will. So she gave them time to sit and chat with
each other to get to know one another a little. The

class dismissed, and they all filed out of the room like rats jumping off the sinking ship. Lorna and Phillip never spoke a word to each other and only shared quick glances. They both went different directions as Lorna went back to her dorm.

Of course, when she got there, no Connie again, but she at least picked up her clothes this time.

Lorna got out her books and started to do her homework. She had just gotten started when the door opened and in walked Connie with two other girls. They were loud; they were all drinking, and smelled like smoke. Lorna looked up at them, then over at Connie, and said: "I'm trying to study, will you please keep it down?"

Connie looked over at Lorna and in a slurred tone said," Come and join us, live a little. It's all you do is study." Then all three of the girls laughed at the same time.

Lorna said, "I have to do my homework. I don't like to drink. With a wrinkled nose she told them "I don't like the smell or taste of beer."

"Okay, your loss! Don't say I didn't invite you." Looking at the other girls and giggling, one of them said under her breath, "what a nerd," and they laughed again.

Lorna's feelings were hurt. She reached over and grabbed her books, piling them all on top of each other. She grabbed her coat, slid on her shoes, and then left. Connie never noticed she was gone. Lorna walked across campus to the library. When she got there, it wasn't packed. It was very quiet and just the way she liked it. Finding a seat, she set her stuff down and hung her coat on the back of a chair. She sat down and reached over, turning the light on that was mounted to the table. She then dove head first into her homework. She'd sat there so long it was now dark outside. Lorna was in her little world and she didn't realize that the library was almost empty.

She got up and moved to the card catalog to find a book she needed. Pulling out drawer after drawer, thumbing through card after card, "ahhh, there you are," she thought. Pulling up the card, she quickly jotted down the information. She placed it back and pushed the draw closed. Walking to the very back of the library, she looked for N332, searching up and down the aisles of books. She finally found it and pulled it off the shelf, muttering under her breath, "Thank goodness for the Dewey Decimal system." Turning around to walk back to her seat, she almost bumped right into Phillip, who standing there watching her. Almost dropping the book, with wide eyes and clutching her heart, the startled Lorna said, "Phillip, what are you doing here?"

Phillip stood there looking at Lorna and with desperation in his voice said, "I seen you in here. I want to talk to you."

"I have nothing to say to you Phillip so please move," as her eyes trailed to the floor.

"I'm not going anywhere until I have a chance to talk to you."

"No, I have nothing to say to you, please move." Lorna stepped to the side to go around him. Phillip stepped right in front of her. She quickly moved to the other side and Phillip again moved in front of her so that she couldn't pass by him.

"Lorna, please, can we talk?" He started walking forward toward Lorna as she started backing up. Phillip kept walking toward her until Lorna's back bumped into the wall. Phillip was now face-to-face with her in the back of the library.
They stood there staring at each other as though they were the only two people left of civilization.

Lorna's eyes puddled up with tears. With a shaky voice and tears streaming down her cheeks she said, "Where were you, Phillip? Why didn't you come back home to me?"

Phillip drew his hand up to Lorna's face, gently took his thumb and slowly wiped the tears from her cheeks. Then he slid his hands up around her face, under her ears, and slowly leaned in to softly kissed her lips. Lorna quickly turned her head to the left, then to the right, and Phillip wouldn't let go, cascading kisses gently all over her face and up and down her neck.

"Phillip, please don't! You hurt me. You HURT ME!" With the tears still running down her cheeks, she tried to push Phillip off of her.

Phillip placed his finger on her lips and said, "Shhh, please don't cry. Lorna, I love you. I love you, Lorna! I've loved you from the day you dumped food all over me. It feels so good to be able to say that out loud to you. Lorna, I've always loved you. I have thought about you every day since I've been gone. Lorna, can you ever forgive me for hurting you?" Phillip leaned in to kiss her again.

Lorna, with a shocked look on her face, said "You love me?"

"Yes! I love you with all my heart and I can't go another day on this campus and not tell you. When I saw you that day of registration on the steps, I honestly thought I saw things. I can't tell you how happy I was when I saw you. I thought you'd feel the same way but then you ran away. I don't understand why. I even told your friend Connie that I had a girlfriend because in my heart you're my girlfriend and always have been. I haven't been with any other girl since I was with you Lorna." He leaned his face beside her cheek and Lorna could feel her face getting wet with his tears.

She backed him up and looked him in the eyes. As the tears fell from both their eyes, Lorna said, "If you loved me that much how could you hurt me like that? Phillip, I don't understand what happened, why didn't you come back to me."

Phillip backed up, then looked Lorna in her eyes and said, "I'm confused, I thought…" Lorna cut him off in mid-sentence saying with eyebrows pushed together, "What? You thought if you could get me vulnerable and kiss me like this that I'd give in and forgive what you did to me?"

"Lorna, I truly regret what I have done to you. I love you so much! What can I do to make this better? For you to forgive me?"

Lorna stood there watching the expression on Phillip's face and the desperation in his voice. Phillip is so handsome, she thought. With her voice scornful and angry, she said, "Look, Phillip, there is no fixing this or us. What you have done to me is unforgivable."

"Lorna, I'm sorry! How many times can I say that until you believe it? I don't understand! Other than me not calling you or coming back home, why are you so mad at me?"

"You used me, Phillip, you used me!" she whispered under her breath as the tears welled back up in her eyes.

"WHAT THE HELL ARE YOU TALKING ABOUT?" he shouted, as anger flew from his eyes.

"Your journal, Phillip! I read it. You wrote that you were using me as a pawn in a twisted game you were playing with your father to get your way and come to this college and study to be a doctor. I read it with my own eyes! You used me, Phillip. Now you're standing in front of me professing your undying love for me and I'm supposed to believe you! You never called, wrote or came home since the day you left."

"Lorna, I couldn't do any of that. The agreement that Father and I made was that he'd let me come to this college to become a doctor but I was never to contact you again. He said he was going to have me watched to make sure I didn't try to contact you. I had to sign a contract with him. If I broke that contract he said I'd be completely cut off of any money and I'd have to pay for school myself. So, yes, I'm guilty of choosing my career over us, but I've regretted it every single minute of every day since."

"Even when your father called and told you that I was having your baby, you still didn't come home or call. Why Phillip? Where were you? Where were you when I buried our daughter? WHERE WERE YOU? I didn't know if you were dead or alive!" Lorna dropped her book on the floor and pounded on Phillips' chest with both of her fists. She was crying so hard her shoulders were bobbing up and down.

Phillip backed up grabbed ahold of both her hands to stop her from hitting him and said, "Wh...what the FUCK are you talking about?" He shook his head, running his perfectly manicured fingers across his face and through his hair. He said, "Let me get this straight...you were pregnant with my baby and then she died. You buried our daughter?"

"Yes, Phillip, that's what I'm saying."

Phillip stood there looking at Lorna in shock with his mouth perched open. He placed his hands on his hips and paced back in forth. Phillip leaned against the wall, then slid all the way down until his butt hit the floor. He tilted his head back, closed his eyes, and the tears ran down his face.

Phillip opened his tear-soaked eyes and said to Lorna, "I had no idea. Honest to God, Lorna, I didn't know that you were pregnant." Phillip begged her to tell him everything. He sat on the floor of the library with his back against the wall, arms resting on his bent knees and fingers intertwined with hers as the tears fell from his eyes.

Lorna, sitting on the floor with him, then said, "After you left for school, about six weeks later I found out I was pregnant. My dad threw me out. Then my dad took me to the doorstep of your father's house. At that point, your father invited me to move in and said he'd care for me until I had the baby. He said it would disgrace your family name if anyone found out I was pregnant with your baby. Then your father removed me from school and I did all of my senior year at your father's house. While I was there, that's when I read your journal. Your father told me that he'd told you that I was pregnant. I ask him if you were coming home for

Christmas. Your father told me you said you weren't coming back for Christmas and you were going skiing with some friends you'd meet at school."

"Then, when I went into labor, the baby was coming out the wrong way. She was breech, which means she was coming out feet first instead of head first. The doctor had to do an emergency C-section on me to get the baby out. When I woke up in the hospital room, the doctor told me that our little girl had died during delivery. He said the cord wrapped around her neck and she was already gone before they even got her out. I named her Mary. Your family and mine walked our daughter to the gravesite and buried her." Lorna expelled a deep breath as the tears fell from her eyes. Wiping the tears from her face she said, "Phillip, that was the hardest thing I've ever had to do and you were nowhere around."

Phillip, leaning against the wall with his hands resting against his mouth and as tears fell from his eyes kept saying in a whisper, "You bastard. You bastard!" He swallowed hard, cleared his throat and sat up, sliding across the floor over to Lorna. He took his finger, touching her chin, and lifted her head up to eye level.

He looked deep into her big, blue, tear-soaked eyes and said, "I swear to you, Lorna, I had no idea that you lived in my house and you were pregnant with my baby. My father and I haven't spoken a word to each other since I left Yale. My father lied to you, Lorna. I honestly don't know what to do or say to make this better."

"Well, I'm much better than I was. I talked to the pastor of my church and he made me feel better, but there isn't a day that goes by that I don't think of her or still feel her." Lorna stood up, lifted her dress, and revealed the scar to Phillip from the C-section. Phillip put his hand on her stomach and traced the scare with his index finger. He moved closer to Lorna. He wrapped his arms around Lorna's waist, laid his head against her stomach, hugged her tight and cried convulsively. Lorna stood there with her hands on Phillip until he stood up and wrapped his arms around her, hugging her so close.

Phillip took a deep breath and with his face full of pain he said, "Lorna, did you see her? Was she as beautiful as you? I would've been there for you Lorna had I known. I am so truly sorry you had to go through that alone. I'm sorry my baby Mary! Daddy didn't know about you and I wasn't there for your Mommy! Rest in peace baby girl." Lorna laid her head on his shoulder and cried her heart out.

Lorna told Phillip she never got to see the baby, that the doctor took her, and his father made all the arrangements for the funeral. They buried her, but she never got to see her. Lorna told Phillip how it was so weird and that right to that day it was like she could still almost feel her baby. It was as though she was still alive and that sometimes she thought she could hear her crying.

Phillip leaned his head sideways and kissed the top of her head. Lorna looked up, then Phillip leaned in slowly and softly kissed her lips. He slowly placed feather like kisses on her wet, salty face, and then all over her neck. While the both of them were still crying, Phillip kept telling Lorna how sorry he was and how much he loved her. Phillip started running his hands up and down Lorna's body and the feeling was like electricity. She hadn't been with anyone since Phillip and the sensation was almost too much to bear.

Lorna leaned into Phillip, feeling the full length of his body against hers. She started kissing him passionately. Laying kisses all over his face and neck, her breath was labored and warm. Phillip could tell she wanted more of him. He ran his hands over her covered breast and slowly up and down her body. Phillip slid his hand down her skirt to the bottom. While softly placing whisper kisses on her face, he slid his hand up her skirt to her panties. Phillip caressed her tight, firm butt and moved around to the front. He placed his hand on her, cradled her in his palm and slowly moved his hand back and forth, massaging her through her panties. Lorna let out a moan and he slowly slid his hand up and down inside of her panties. Lorna slowly dropped her arms and voluntarily moved her legs apart. Phillip took his finger and entered her. Lorna arched her back, tilting her head back against the wall with her eyes closed and anticipation building inside of her. She made soft throaty sounds while he touched her, trying to swallow, and not able to catch her breath. "Ahhh… this feeling is so amazing," Lorna thought. She lost all control to Phillips' hand, her body starting to shake, and she released herself and exploded inside.

Phillip slowly moved his hand away when he knew Lorna was finished and slid her panties down her legs. As they softly hit the floor, he undid the zipper of his pants and removed himself. He lifted Lorna up against the wall as she straddled her legs around him. Phillip slowly entered Lorna. Lorna could feel him fill her insides. Holding onto her by her butt, breathing heavily, he kissed Lorna long and hard. He picked up rhythm moving in and out of her until he spilled his seed inside of her. He leaned his head against Lorna's and said with his breath labored, "I love you so much, Lorna."

Lorna hugged him tight and said, "I love you, too." Phillip pulled himself away from Lorna and adjusted himself. Lorna bent down and put her panties back on.

Phillip backed her up a little and said, "I have a question. You said you read my journal. Did you read all of it or just some of it?"

"Just a few pages, enough to know what you'd done, then I put it back in your drawer. Why?"

"Because if you would've read more of it you would've found a poem I wrote for you called 'A Letter to a Friend.' I told you in that entry how much I loved you and how sorry I was."

Lorna said, "Really? I never saw that."

"Yes, and the day my father decided to let me come to this college, I had put my class ring on a chain and I was going to give it to you to wear. I put it back in the box on my dresser because I knew I couldn't be with you, that I had to let you go."

Lorna said, "Wow, really?" As she quickly reflected to being in Phillips room, she remembered holding that chain in her hand while the ring dangled from it.

"I believe you, Phillip, I do." She wrapped her arms around him and told him she loved him. Phillip put his arms around her waist leaning in and kissing her softly on the lips.

Just then the librarian came around the corner saw them embraced in each other's arms. She cleared her throat, stating in a soft voice, "Excuse me, I don't mean to interrupt you, but the library is closing and I'm going to have to ask you to leave."

Lorna and Phillip looked up at this woman in her late forties with brown hair pulled up in a tight bun and wearing cat-eye glasses.

Lorna and Phillip dropped their arms from each other. Lorna picked up her book and they walked up front. Lorna gathered all her stuff, checked out her book, and Lorna and Phillip left the library together. Phillip leaned in and whispered to Lorna, "If that librarian had come around that corner any sooner she would've gotten an eyeful," and then he laughed out loud.

With a sheepish smile, Lorna snickered a little, and Phillip walked her to her dorm. They said goodnight.

The Settlement

Chapter 4

Lorna woke up early the next day while it was still dark outside. She rolled over on her side, tucking her hands under her face on the pillow. Staring at an empty bed across the room from her, she realized Connie never came home. With a pit forming in her stomach, she could feel something was wrong. Trying to brush off that feeling, Lorna laid there thinking about the night before with Phillip, then a smile came across her face involuntarily. Her heart was full again, then she thought of Theodore Powell and the arrangement she'd made with that awful, despicable man. With chills running down her spine, she knew she still had to tell Phillip what happened and how she ended up at the University of Michigan.

Lorna rolled over on her back with still an unsettling feeling that something was wrong. She let out a big sigh, threw off the covers and got out of bed. Lorna didn't have any classes on Friday, deciding to do some homework while the room was still quiet. With her books spread all over, she studied for a couple of hours until she got all her homework done. She cleaned up the room, took a shower, and left to get something to eat. While walking to the cafeteria, Phillip walked up beside her and slid his hand into her hand.

Lorna quickly looked up at him, then smiled. He asked if she would like to go somewhere else to eat and spend the day together. Lorna was more than thrilled to accompany Phillip for the day. They walked hand in hand to his car. As usual, Phillip was a gentleman. He opened her door, and Lorna slid into the seat. Phillip
ran around to the driver's side, slipped into his seat looking over at Lorna, and then said, "Where to, my queen?"

Lorna laughed, then said, "It's up to you. I have no idea where to go or what to do. I've never been to Ann Arbor." Running her hand across the dashboard, she thought with nostalgia about the last time she was in Phillip's car; it was the last time she'd seen him.

"Ok, well, we both want to eat breakfast so let's find a restaurant and eat first." Phillip drove around and then down to Catherine Street and found Angelo's Restaurant. The restaurant was already busy and they were seated in the back. Angelo's was relatively new, and everyone was

trying out the new spot in town. The walls were
white ceramic tile with black square tiles making a
border around the ceiling, stainless steel counters,
and pictures on the walls of things from around
Michigan. They ordered their breakfast of eggs,
bacon, toast and hot coffee. They laughed and
talked, just enjoying each other's company. A
couple of times Lorna became really quiet and
Phillip noticed, asking if she was ok. Lorna had
told him that she woke up with an awful feeling that
something was wrong. Phillip asked if Lorna had
called home to check on her family? She told him
she'd do it when they get back to the school. They
both left the restaurant stuffed and Phillip patted
his stomach on the way out the door.

They held hands walking up and down the streets
and did some window shopping. Halloween was in
a week, and all the windows were dressed for
harvest. Big orange pumpkins everywhere and the
air was fresh and brisk. Lorna knew it wouldn't be
long before it started to snow. She hung on tight to
Phillip's hand as
they walked around town. Lorna looked up and
saw The State Theatre where The Ten
Commandments starring Charlton Heston was
playing.

"Oh, Phillip," she says "Can we go see it?" with a
girlish look on her face.

"Yes, of course, we can. Is this really about the Ten Commandments from the Bible? "If so, I'm going to be completely lost," he said, with reluctance on his face.

"Yes, Phillip, it's literally about the Bible's Ten Commandments. It will be ok; I'll tell you what it all means," she told him with a broad smile.

They bought their tickets and went inside and found a seat. From the minute the movie started, Phillip kept looking over at Lorna. She never took her eyes off the screen or barley blinked.

When the movie ended, they left. Phillip was so full of questions, wanting to know why this and why that. Lorna answered as best she could. Phillip told her that it was an excellent movie and he'd learned a lot of things he didn't know about the Bible.

They held hands and spent the rest of the day walking around just taking in the sights. The weather was perfect for snuggling with each other. They went down Woodbury Drive. They checked out all the stores. They stopped for hot cocoa to go and walked down to Burns Park, then found a park bench to settle into and enjoyed the beauty. The trees were an array of different colors. Lorna told Phillip that Fall was her favorite time of the year. He said it was his too, the colors of the leaves on the trees so brilliant and how they'd fall to the ground with such grace and elegance it almost left you breathless.

They sat on the bench not saying a word, just enjoying each other's presence. They watched kids playing in the piles of leaves, people riding their bikes, people
walking their dogs, and a Dad playing catch with his little boy. Lorna hooked her arm into Phillip's and snuggled in tight to him. With both her hands wrapped around her cup, she sipped her hot cocoa.

Lorna thought she never wanted that day to end; she wanted to stay tucked into Phillip for the rest of her life where she felt safe and complete.

Phillip said to Lorna, "Are you cold?" as he pulled her closer to him.

"Yes, a little," she said, laying her head on his shoulder.

Looking down at her, Phillip asked, "Do you want to go?"

"No, but we probably should. I need to make a call to my family anyway." She lifted her head and they both stood up. They made it back to the car, and Phillip turned on the heat to warm Lorna up.

They drove back to the school and returned to reality. The radio was playing a ballet by Five Satins, "In the Still of the Nite." Lorna put her hand on Phillips, squeezing a little, and she told him she had had a wonderful day. She reached up and turned the radio down. Lorna told Phillip she was so glad that he was back in her life. Phillip smiled and said he was thrilled as well. Lorna's stomach flipped when she told him she needed to tell him something, something that would change everything for the rest of his life. Phillip quickly glanced over at Lorna with an arched eyebrow and said, "Well, I surely don't like the sound of that." He returned his eyes to the road.

Lorna was so nervous she could hardly talk! She took a deep breath and started to speak as they pulled around the corner to the school. They both saw two police cars out front of her dorm. Lorna gasped, covering her mouth. Her stomach somersaulted. "I knew… Oh gosh, I knew there was something wrong."
Phillip grabbed her hand, gently squeezed, and then said, "Calm down, you don't know what happened yet." Phillip quickly pulled up behind the police car. The car had barely stopped when Lorna jumped out. She started to run up to the door, forgetting Phillip was with her.
Phillip parked the car and rushed up to Lorna. A police officer was standing at the entrance of the door. Lorna whipped the door open and rushed inside. Phillip wasn't allowed to go into her dorm so he stood outside waiting for Lorna to come back.

"What happened?" Lorna said in a breathless tone.

The police officer looked at her and said, "We're looking for the roommate of Connie Davis. Do you know who that might be?"

"Me...that's me. Oh my gosh what happened? Where is Connie? Is she ok?" She held her hand over her mouth as the tears started to form in her eyes. The police officer said, "Come with me," taking her by the forearm and guiding her back to her room. Walking in, there were two officers in her room going through all of Connie's stuff and some of hers. Looking shocked, Lorna said, "What's going on? Why are you searching through mine and Connie's stuff? Is she in trouble? What happened?"

"Miss, you might want to sit down. We need to ask you some questions." Reaching into the front pocket of his police uniform, the officer pulled out a small pad of paper and a pencil. Flipping it open, he cleared his throat, then said, "What is your full name?"

By this time, Lorna was so scared and crying she said in a shaky voice, "Lorna Jean Collins." She watched the officer write on his little pad of paper.

While gazing at Lorna, he asked with a sharp, stern voice, "How long have you known Connie Davis?"

"I've only known her since the end of August. We both came here almost at the same time to start school."

"How well do you know her?" He placed the pencil tip in his mouth and stared at Lorna as though she were on trial.

"Not that well. I've already told you that I meet Connie in August. We share a dorm room together and a couple of classes. She, too, is studying to be a pediatrician like myself," she said in a sarcastic tone while wiping the tears from her face.

"Did you ever go to any parties with her on campus?" Lorna had to think real quick.

"No, not really. Before school started we'd visited a few of the frat houses. I didn't drink though, I don't like the smell...it's awful."

"Did you ever see Connie smoke cigarettes or anything else?"

"What? No! Of course not! Sir, what is this all about. Is Connie ok?"

"Your friend was in a car crash early this morning. She just has a few bumps and bruises and she's going to be fine. She is now sitting in the county jail for possession of marijuana and being intoxicated on campus grounds."

Lorna let out a gasp, covering her mouth, and whispered under her breath, "I KNEW it. I just knew she was doing something else," she said, looking downcast at the floor.

"Is there something you'd like to add?"

"No, I'm sorry I was just thinking out loud."

With a shred of doubt that flickered across his face, he said, "Are you sure? Because now is the time to tell me."

"Well, I'd noticed that Connie was acting weird the last couple of weeks. I had a feeling she was doing something she shouldn't have been."

"What made you think that?" he questioned, tapping his pencil on his pad of paper.

"Because she was staying out late all the time, missing classes, and was gone whenever I'd come back here after class. So what now? What is going to happen to her?"

"I'm not sure. I can almost assure you that Connie will be expelled from this college. They have zero tolerance for such behavior. As far as the drug charge, that will be up to the judge."

Lorna's heart sank into her gut because she felt so sorry for Connie. Lorna thought that if she'd said something sooner to someone then maybe none of this would've of happened.

The police officers were finished now. They gathered up what they needed, and the officer that was questioning Lorna handed her a card. He said, "This is my contact number. If there's anything else you can think of that might help, please call me at that number." He handed the card to Lorna.

Lorna took the card and stared at it in disbelief. She looked at his name and said, "Officer Jensen?

Could you please tell Connie that I'm so sorry that this happened to her?"

"When I see her again, yes!" He tucked his pad of paper and pencil back into his shirt pocket. When the officers left her room, Lorna sat down on her bed with her heart broken for Connie and thought how she must be so scared. Lorna let out a

heavy sigh and decided to clean up the room. Just as Lorna stood up, at that moment, a wave came over her. Phillip! Oh my gosh, Phillip! She ran out the door and down to Phillip. He was still there, leaning up against the wall with his hands tucked in his pockets. Lorna rushed over to him, threw her arms around him, and just cried. He hugged her tight.

He said, "Lorna, is everything ok?"

Lorna sniffed and backed up and told him what had happened. Phillip stood there with his jaw hanging open. He couldn't believe what he was hearing. He said, "You mean that girl I met in the cafeteria that day? The same girl that asked me out?" He stared at Lorna with disbelief on his face.

"Yes, that's her. Connie was my roommate. Now she's going to be expelled from school and she's facing drug charges."

"Wow, I never would have thought that from her. I'm in total shock. I'm sorry Lorna, I know she was your friend."

"I hardly knew her, but I knew she was doing more than drinking. She acted high all the time. She was missing class all the time and staying out all night. Phillip, if I would've gone with my gut instinct and talked to someone about this, then maybe, just maybe, none of this would've happened."

"Lorna, you can't blame yourself for this. Nothing would've stopped her and, besides, then she would've been mad at you."

"I wouldn't have cared. That would've been a risk I would've been willing to take. Now Connie's whole life will change forever, and I might have been able to stop that from happening."

"Please, Lorna, it doesn't help to beat yourself up," Phillip said with a sorrowful tone.

Lorna told Phillip she was going to go in and clean up the mess the officers made in her room. She apologized for cutting their evening short. Lorna wasn't in the mood to be around anyone right now. She hugged him tight, then stood on her tiptoes and leaned in and kissed him.

Phillip kissed her back, then said, "Wasn't there something you wanted to talk to me about?"

Lorna stared at him for a second and said, "Another time," knowing she wasn't in the mood to ruin his life, too. She knew she'd had to tell him about his horrible father, but not yet, at least not tonight. Connie was enough for her in one night.

With a somber expression, Phillip said, "Ok, tomorrow is Saturday. Do you want to do something?"

"Umm, I think I need to stay here tomorrow. The police might come back or need me to answer more questions." With tears in her eyes, Lorna asked lightly, in a saintly tone, "What I'd like to do, Phillip, is go to church Sunday. I saw a church just down the road I'd like to attend. What do you think? Would you like to go with me?" she asked him, looking at him in despair.

Phillip looked bewildered at Lorna's flawless beauty and said "Yes, for you, Lorna, I'd walk across hot coals. Of course, I'll go to church with you. What time does service start?" he asked, smiling wryly.

Lorna's eyes twinkled and her face lit up. "Really Phillip? You'll go to church with me?"

"Yes, of course I will."

"That would be swell. Thank you! Thank you, Phillip! Service starts at 9:30." Lorna was so excited.

I'll see you Sunday then. Good night Lorna."

"That will be perfect. I'll see you then. I love you Phillip." Leaning in, she kissed him again, turned around and walked away.

Phillip said, "I love you too, Lorna!" Looking melancholy, he watched her walk away.

Lorna later learned that Connie was expelled from the University of Michigan for violating the rules and put on probation for six months. She never heard from Connie again, but Lorna often wondered about her and didn't ever forget her.

The Settlement

Chapter 5

Lorna got up early Sunday morning and could hear the rain hitting the window. She showered and readied herself for church. Lorna was wearing a cute, dark brown and yellow fall dress with sunflowers, a yellow sweater, and brown and white saddle shoes. Sitting by the window, she watched for Phillip. The rain was a steady fall drizzle that put her in a trance. Lorna remembered back to when she and Phillip first met and how they'd shared the most incredible summer of her life, how she had fallen in love with him and then he left her, and her stomach flipped. Would she ever be able to look upon the past again without feeling sick about it, she wondered.

Just then, she saw Phillip's black car pull up out front. Grabbing her coat, Bible and umbrella, she raced out the door and down to Phillip. He jumped out of the car, holding his hand in front of his face to block the rain. He ran around to the other side to open the door for Lorna. Phillip was in a dark brown suit with a tie and he looked and smelled delicious she thought. Phillip said good morning to her and told her she looked beautiful. Smiling sheepishly, Lorna said, "Thank you, and you look very nice yourself."

"Ok, let's do this," Phillip said, laying his hand on hers. With his eyes fixed on the road, "I don't know what to do in a church, Lorna, and I'm ashamed to say that out loud."

"It will be fine. Just follow me and I'll show you what to do," she told him, squeezing his hand gently.

They arrived at a Lutheran Church. Lorna went to a Baptist Church back home, so this was a little different for her. She didn't care, though, as long as she was there and having Phillip with her was such a blessing. They were greeted at the door with smiles and handshakes. They took a seat and service started with songs from the hymn book. Phillip held the book. Lorna never looked down once to see the music for she knew every note by heart. The piano player played the song, Amazing Grace, by John Newton. After they all took a seat, Pastor Ron stood in front of the congregation and asked everyone to take out their Bibles and turn to the book of Matthew 2:14. He then began to preach.

When service was over, Phillip and Lorna rose and headed for the door. Everyone shook their hands and welcomed them to the church. Pastor Ron made it a point to say hello and told them it was nice to see new young faces in the church. Phillip took the umbrella from Lorna, popped it open, and they hustled to the car.

Phillip went to pull away but stopped and put the car in park. He looked at Lorna and said, "I thoroughly enjoyed that and I want to know more. With a voice full of compassion, he told Lorna, "I want you to teach me about the God you're in love with."

Lorna's eyes sprung wide with disbelief and she replied, "Wh...what? Oh, Phillip, that would be swell! Of course! I'll teach you everything I know." Phillip smiled, revealing his perfect charm.

They spent the rest of the day together. They ate lunch at the Old Town Tavern. Phillip had been there before with some friends and had had the most fantastic cheeseburger so he wanted Lorna to try one. The place was crowded and loud, but the food was worth it. They talked and watched it rain. Phillip asked Lorna what else she wanted to do and she told him she needed to get back. She had laundry and needed to get ready for class in the morning. Phillip pulled up in front of the dorm. Lorna turned sideways in the car, looked at Phillip, and she thanked him for such a beautiful day. He slid his hand around her face and Lorna stared into his beautiful green eyes. Phillip leaned in and softly laid a kiss on her lips. The radio was down low and the song "My Prayer" by the Platters was on and they kissed and listened to the words.

Lorna took his hand and said to Phillip, "That's my prayer that you'll still there when my prayer is over."

Phillip laid his index finger lightly on Lorna's soft lips and ordered her to shush. "I promise, Lorna, I'm not going anywhere. Someday, I will make you my wife, and we will live in Yale together. I will open my practice in town and we will be together," he said, with sparkling eyes and enthusiasm in his voice.

Lorna sat listening to Phillip talk about their future. It gave her such warmth, but she was still scared. Lorna wasn't sure she could trust Phillip with her heart.

She smiled at Phillip and with wide eyes said, "Darling, you've got this all figured out."

"Yes, my love, I do. I've been thinking about this for a long time. I promised myself that if I was ever lucky enough to get you back I was never letting you go, despite what Father thinks." He held her hand up to her face and kissed her fingers very gently.

Lorna thought of her "arrangement" she had made with Phillip's father. She still had to tell Phillip about the whole thing. "Phillip, my darling, there's something I must tell you."

Phillip rested his face against her hand and looked deep into her bright blue eyes. He closed his eyes and lightly ran his hand up and down her face, kissing her fingers. His eyes flickered slightly and Phillip looked seductively at her. Lorna was so caught up in what he was doing to her that the moment of telling him about his cruel father passed.

He leaned in, kissed her again on the lips, moved up and down her neck, and then all over her face.

Lorna sat with her eyes closed caught up in the moment. She pulled herself away and said, "Phillip, stop. We have nowhere to go. I believe the library's closed," she giggled.

A smile flickered across his lips. Looking up at her with an arched eyebrow, Phillip took Lorna's hand and gently kissed her fingers again, lightly sucking on her fingertips. He pulled back and said, "I have an idea. You have a room with a bed. We've never been together in a bed. You're all alone in there. I think we should go inside."

"Phillip, you know that you can't come in there. We will both be in big trouble if we get caught." She slowly pulled her hand back and rested it on her lap. With a look of lust in her eyes, she glanced at Phillip and said, "Okay, let's do it!"

"Cool," Phillip said, reaching over to open his door.
They ran through the rain and up to the door.
Lorna stopped, turned to Phillip, and said, "Shh....we have to be quiet." She opened the door and they both went inside. They darted down the hall as Lorna heard someone talking and getting closer to them.

"Quick! Hide! Someone is coming!" she told him in a panicked voice.

Phillip quickly looked around then hid behind the curtains in the hall. The two girls talking and laughing passed by Lorna, smiled, said hello, and kept going. When it was all clear, she told Phillip to come out. Lorna looked over at the curtain. She could see Phillip's feet sticking out. She giggled to herself, thinking "I never thought I'd see the day that Phillip Powell was hiding behind curtains in a girl's dorm." Phillip quickly popped out from behind the curtain. She unlocked the door to her room and they went in. Lorna quickly closed the door and they removed their coats. Phillip stood in the middle of the room looking around. Sliding his hands in his pockets, he took a tour around her little room, picking up things and setting them down. He asked what bed was hers, and she pointed to the other side of the room. Phillip walked over and sat down. Lorna went over to her record player and pulled out an album of Frank Sinatra. She set it on the turntable, lifted the arm, and set the needle down. The record crackled and Frank Sinatra started to sing, "I Got a Crush on You." Lorna turned to look at Phillip. She placed her arms around to her back and hooked her fingers together. She swayed back in forth, closing her eyes and humming his song.

Phillip watched her. He got up and glided smoothly and quickly across to her. Lorna watched with seduction in her eyes as Phillip moved closer to her. He walked up to her, standing in front of her face-to-face. He put his hands on her shoulders and slid his hands down her arms, bringing her hands around to the front of her. He hooked his hands in hers, leaned in, and gently kissed her lips. He let go of one side then swirled her around in a circle and brought her in close to him with her back against his chest. He pulled her hand and she moved back out to stand in front of him. He swirled and twirled her back and forth, bringing her in close to his face. He stood there looking into her bright blue eyes, placed one hand on her side just above her hip, and then slid his other hand into her hand. He brought it up close to his chest and moved side to side and around in a circle, putting his cheek next to hers while singing softly in her ear.

"I'm your big and brave and handsome Romeo
How I won you, I shall never never know
It's not that you're attractive
But, oh, my heart grew active
When you came into view

I've got a crush on you, sweetie pie
All the day and night-time give me sigh
I never had the least notion that
I could fall with so much emotion."

   Pulling her closer, he whispered in her ear, "I've
got a crush on you." He leaned her backward so
her long blonde hair cascaded toward the floor.
Phillip slowly brought her back up to his face.
Lorna was winded from dancing and breathing
heavy into Phillip's face, she smiled and leaned in to
kiss Phillip long and seductively. Phillip slid both of
his hands up around her face, brought her in closer,
and cascaded soft butterfly kisses across her face.
He embraced her body next to his. Feeling the
warmth of Lorna's body next to his aroused him.

   He tenderly rubbed up and down her body slowly.
He slid his hand up the back of her dress and slowly
unzipped it down to her waist. Taking his hands up

to her shoulders, he hooked his fingers around the dress and slid the dress down her arms seductively.
Lorna's dress fell into a soft pile around her feet on the floor. He reached up her back and unhinged her white bra, provocatively letting it fall to the floor. He slid his hands down her sultry body, then pushed her white panties down her legs and they drifted to the floor. Lorna stepped out of her shoes, then moved the clothes aside. Lorna reached up, took Phillip's jacket off, and let it drop to the floor. Looking Phillip in the eyes, she slowly undid his tie, pulled it out from around the neck of his shirt, and threw it on the floor. Lorna leaned in, giving a long kiss, putting her tongue in his mouth, and they explored each other passionately.

Reaching her hand up, Lorna started to unbutton his shirt, one button at a time. She slid her hands upon his bare chest, running her fingers all over his body. She leaned in with alluring eyes staring at him and flirtatiously nibbled on his bottom lip.
Gliding her hands down to his belt, she undid it and the button of his pants. She unzipped his zipper and with both hands freed his pants and boxers at the same time, letting them fall to the floor. Phillip removed his shoes and stepped out of his clothes. Taking Lorna by the fingertips, Phillip guided her to the bed.

Lorna laid down on the bed and moved her perfect, small frame over. Phillip laid next to her. He leaned down and gently kissed Lorna's lips, slid his hand up her stomach to her perky young breasts, cupping first one and then the other in his hands. Moving his head down, he licked her erect nipple, closed his lips around it and nibbled gently. Lorna let out a moan. Gliding his tongue across her bare body was electrifying to Lorna and stimulated her in a way that made her arch her back. Phillip moved down her body, down to her inner thigh, seductively trailing soft kisses between her legs. He parted her legs, bent her knees slightly, and moved up to her desirably wet area. Running his tongue across her, he touched her intimately, moving his tongue around it slowly. Lorna about lost it right there in his mouth! She clutched her fingers into the sheets of her bed. She tilted her head back and with eyes closed, arched her back and took in a deep breath.

Phillip's tongue explored her inner self intimately. Moving his tongue around in little circles, up and down, darting in and out of her. As Phillip washed Lorna with his tongue, she bucked her hips up and down in erotic pleasure. It was a pleasure she'd never known before. Releasing one hand from the bed, she grabbed ahold of Phillips head and pulled him in tighter to her. The desire was uncontrollable. Lorna moaned, breathing heavily, making soft sounds in her throat. She tilted her head back as far as it would go and arched her back with an explosion she couldn't hold back any longer. She released herself on Phillip. Letting out her breath slowly, she collapsed her body feeling like Jell-O. She laid herself down on the bed.

Phillip slowly moved up her long bare body until he was on top of her. Kissing her passionately, Lorna still breathing heavy, she wrapped her arms around Phillip. Telling her she smells intoxicating, he nibbles on her earlobe, down the side of her neck, and finally to her breast again. He moved his body down, put his mouth on her breasts and licked, first one and then the other. Now sensitive to his touch, Lorna's body gave into Phillip again. He reached down between her legs and guided himself inside of her. Gently, he slid himself in and out of her. Lorna was overcome with pleasure again. Phillip collapsed his body halfway down on her and Lorna coiled her legs around his bare frame.

He moved and Lorna picked up his rhythm. They moved together like a perfect row of geese flying south for the winter. Lorna's breathing was labored. She slid her hands down to his butt and applied pressure, urging Phillip to move faster and faster. Lorna thought, "Oooo... it can't be happening again!" With sensations building up inside of her, she lost all her senses and released herself on Phillip. He pumped a few more times and released his seed inside of Lorna. He completely collapsed on top of Lorna, breathing heavily. They laid there embraced in each other arms with their hearts beating in sync.

Phillip pushed himself up and stared into Lorna's eyes. His breath was still labored and his eyes were soft. He murmured, "I love you so much, Lorna. I promise that someday I'll make you my wife." Leaning down, he pressed his lips to hers and kissed her long, showing her his love and compassion. He removed himself from her and fell sideways on her bed.

Lorna reached down to the bottom of the bed and grabbed the blanket, pulling it up and covering both their naked bodies. Phillip rolled onto his back and Lorna snuggled in tight to Phillip. Squeezing him tight in her arms, she said, "I had no idea that making love could be so incredible. I love you, Phillip. This is the happiest I've been in a long time." Phillip pulled her in tight and they laid there listening to Frank Sinatra singing while they both fell asleep.

Lorna woke up startled at around 3 a.m. She listened to the crackling from the record and looked over with Phillip still next to her. Looking around the room, she collected her composer. She moved

Phillip's shoulder, saying softly, "Phillip, get up. You have to get out of here before we get caught."

Phillips' eyes sprung open and he looked at Lorna's beauty beside him. "Holy shit! I have to go!" Rolling over top of Lorna, he rushed to get dressed as Lorna watched his perfect, naked frame moving in the dark with just a glow of light coming from her record player. Lorna got up, put on her panties, then her nightgown, and walked Phillip to the door. They stood there kissing, saying goodbye.

Phillip took her tiny face in his hands, kissed the end of her nose, and looking her deep in the eyes said, "I love you, Lorna. You have made me so happy and complete."

Lorna smiled wide, stating, "Same here. I love you, too, Phillip." She opened the door and Phillip poked his head out to see if the coast was clear. Popping his head back in, he kissed Lorna once more and told her he'd see her shortly for breakfast in the cafeteria. Lorna told him she'd be there and that she couldn't wait. Phillip went out, closed the door, and he was gone.

Lorna set her alarm, curled back into bed. She pulled the blanket close to her face so she could smell his scent on the sheet, closed her eyes, and went to sleep.

The Settlement

Chapter 6

Halloween came and went while Lorna and Phillip spent all their spare time together. Phillip had snuck into Lorna's dorm room so many times he practically lived there. They studied together. They met with Tammy and Scott several times to work on their Chemistry project. Midterms were coming quick but Lorna was studying well in advance for her midterms. She loved school! She was so full of energy and had met some great people. She was grateful to have the opportunity to be at one of the most excellent colleges in the state of Michigan.

Lorna was feeling melancholy with the holidays approaching, remembering harvest time in Yale. Michigan was the place to be at such a beautiful time of year. The brisk, fall smells, apple picking, carving pumpkins, and the farmers clearing their sugar beets, wheat, corn, and soybeans, preparing for winter. Lorna called home several times. Her mom and dad asked if she'd be coming back for Thanksgiving. Lorna told them no, she would be staying at school and she'd be home for Christmas. Lorna didn't want to leave Phillip during Thanksgiving. She hadn't told her parents yet that she and Phillip were back together, out of fear of what they would say. The last time Phillip's name was mentioned in front of her dad, he wanted to choke the life from him for getting his daughter pregnant. She wasn't sure how she was going to tell them or if they'd even believe that he knew nothing at all about her being pregnant. She thought she'd cross that bridge when she got to it.

Winter was coming faster than expected and it had already started to snow. Everything was frozen and bitter cold outside. Phillip was waiting outside the cafeteria for Lorna, looking like a gorgeous statue that someone carved out. He had his hands tucked deep in his front pockets, black leather jacket zipped all the way up, wearing jeans and black boots. Lorna came around the corner, her long blonde hair shining under the cold autumn skies. She saw Phillip standing there and thought to herself, "He looks frozen." She walked up to Phillip, leaning in and kissing his cold lips. "You look frozen and your nose is red," she giggled.

Phillip's teeth were almost chattering together, but he said, "I am, so let's go." He grabbed her hand and led her to his car. He pulled her along by the hand with Lorna yelling breathlessly behind him, "Where are we going?"

"Get in! I have a plan. And it's a plan I think you'll love," he told her as he opened the car door. Phillip ran around to the other side, sliding in. Turning the ignition over and starting the car, he turned the heat all the way up, rubbing his hands together and blowing his hot breath into them. Looking over at Lorna, Phillip paused, then smiled wide and winked at her.

"What, what are we doing?" Lorna said with a smirk on her face.

"Hold on, let me warm up a little. I can't talk yet. I'm too cold." Lorna held her hands in front of the heat vents. She sat still, waiting for Phillip to tell her about the grand plan he'd cooked up.

"Okay. Since neither one of us are going home for Thanksgiving, I've made reservations at the Fisher Hotel in Frankenmuth for next weekend. We will be done with our midterms, so we can relax and have fun. How's that sound? If you don't want to go, we can cancel." He studied her with appraising eyes.

Lorna tossed her long hair away from her face with a whimsical smile. She stared into Phillip's green eyes mesmerized by the flecks of brown within them as the sun shone down upon his face.

Putting her hand on his, Lorna says in a near whisper, "That would be lovely, Phillip. I'd love to go there with you. When did you say we're leaving?" she asked with a smile on her lips.

Phillip said, "Thanksgiving is on Thursday the 22nd, so I thought we'd leave early the Saturday before Thanksgiving. If we go early that morning, we can check in and spend the whole day looking around."

"That sounds amazing! I can't wait," she told him, tucking her hands between her legs.

"Are you sure you don't want to go home for Thanksgiving? You know I'll take you home."

"I'm fine with it, Phillip. I wasn't home last year either for the holidays. I lived in your house," Lorna said in a downcast, pitiful voice.

Phillip was taken off guard, arched his lips into an O, then said, "Oooo that's right! I'm so sorry. I forgot." He glanced sideways at her, almost feeling guilty.

"It's okay; this is all new to you."

Lorna sat staring at Phillip, relishing in his magnificently handsome features. With her eyes, she traced his square, chiseled jaw line, which dominated his even-featured face, and his broad shoulders (he made everything he wore look so good!) And his eyes …… oh, his eyes are so dreamy, she thought.

"As far as today, I thought we'd go to the movies," he told her with a grin on his face.

"Sure, I'd love to! At least it's warm in there. What are we going to see?" Lorna giggled.

"Well, it's a surprise," he said, smiling wily.

"C'mon, tell me. I don't like surprises."

"Too bad! You have to wait. Hold on and you'll know in a few minutes," he said with a smirk.

Lorna sat back in her seat, let out a big sigh and folded her hands in her lap, staring out the window. The scenery looked very familiar to her. Phillip whipped the car into a parking space, hopped out, and walked around to open the door for Lorna. She took his hand and stepped out. Hearing a loud roar from a crowd, she looked up at Phillip.

Puzzled, she rushed to the curb to see what was going on. Lorna saw a line of people, mostly girls, jumping up and down and talking loud. They were standing in front of The State Theatre. Lorna looked up at what was playing and threw her hands over her mouth. "Love Me Tender starring Elvis Presley!" With excitement in her voice and a sparkle in her eyes, she threw her arms around Phillip's neck, squeezing hard. "Thank you! Thank you so much! I'm so excited!" Lorna kissed his cheek then his lips.

They got up to the window and Phillip said to the lady, "Two for Love Me Tender." The lady ripped off two tickets while Phillip paid and they went inside. Phillip asked Lorna if she wanted some popcorn and something to drink. She told him she wasn't that hungry. They went in and found a seat and watched Elvis Presley on the big screen. Lorna hugged up to Phillip the whole time. When the movie was over, Phillip kept singing Elvis' new song.

Love me tender, Love me sweet
Never let me go, you have made my life complete,
and I love you so.

Love me tender, Love me true
All my dreams fulfilled, for my darling I love you,
and I always will.

Lorna, with a big smile on her face, leaned in and kissed Phillip soft and gentle on the lips. Phillip returned the kiss, looked into her big, wide eyes and told her he loved her very much.

A smile flickered across her face when she said, "I've waited so long for you to say that to me. I'll never get sick of hearing it. She thanked him again for taking her to see Elvis' new movie.

"Sure, anything to put that big smile on your face. I guess it's the first time I really thought of this, but if my brother James were still around, he would've loved you. Who knows, just like Elvis and his brother in the movie, maybe James and I could be fighting over the same gal?"

Lorna snickered under her breath, then said, "Oh, Phillip." Chuckling, Lorna told him, "Don't be silly, I only have room in my heart for one fellow... and that's ....Elvis Presley!" Laughing out loud and running away from him, Phillip watched Lorna's long blonde hair shimmer under the brisk November skies. He thought to himself that Lorna was irrefutably the most beautiful women he'd ever laid his eyes on and he was a lucky man indeed.

The rest of their afternoon was spent shopping for Christmas gifts for their families. They went from store to store holding hands and swinging shopping bags. They came to Schlanderer & Sons jewelry store and stopped at the window. Lorna stood admiring the beautiful displays that were so classy.

With a boyish look, Phillip said, "Let's go in."

"Don't be silly. We can stay out here and dream from the window." Lorna looked down at the window and absently put her index finger in her mouth, biting on her fingernail.

Phillip reached up, pulled her hand out of her mouth, and dragged her into the store. He opened the door for Lorna to walk through the entrance. Her eyes roamed all over the store. It was warm and cozy and smelled like cinnamon buns. The diamonds sparkled and shone so brilliantly they almost took her breath away. Phillip watched the expression on Lorna's face as she walked from case to case, sliding her hand across the glass counters, slowly looking down admiring the beautiful rings.

Phillip walked up behind her and slipped his hand up to the small of her back. He turned, kissed her cheek, and asked, "Aren't they lovely?"

Lorna turned her head, looked into Phillip's eyes, and said, "Oh Phillip, they're exquisite! I have never seen anything so beautiful in my whole life."

Phillip pressed his forehead to the side of Lorna's face and whispered, "There's not one diamond in this store that comes close to how beautiful you are." He then kissed her tenderly on the cheek. A salesman came to the counter smiling cheerily.

"Good afternoon! How can I help you today?" he inquired with a warm, pleasant smile on his face.

Phillip said, "Good afternoon to you as well. We'd like to see some engagement rings in the ballpark of a half carat." With excitement in his voice, his eyes twinkled and his face lite up.

Lorna leaned in and asked with pursed lips, "Phillip, what are you doing?" Looking up at Phillip with inquisitive eyes, she studied him for a minute and then returned her eyes to the rings in front of her.

"Honey, it doesn't hurt to look." Phillip quickly looked up, winking conspiratorially at the salesman. He told the salesman, "I need to see something as close to the beauty you see before you in this lovely woman."

The gentleman behind the counter gave a friendly smile and brought out several rings. Laying them out in front of them, Lorna tried on one diamond ring after the other, each one more beautiful than the last. Lorna saw one that she ultimately fell in love with. "Whoa! This is gorgeous!" she said.

It was solid platinum with one center diamond, two baguette diamonds, and sixteen round diamonds. The ring was stunning! Lorna slid it onto her ring finger. The size fit her perfectly on her tiny fingers. She held it up in front of her, admiring its brilliance. She took it off, then laid it back on the black felt, and picked up a few more, trying them on. She went right back to the one she liked. She was so captivated and transfixed by it that she gazed at it like a little kid in a candy shop. Taking the ring off one last time, she lay it down again. She looked at Phillip and smiled. They left the jewelry store, returned to finish shopping, and then headed back to school.

Phillip pulled up in front of the school. He turned to Lorna, telling her, "I'm really sorry, Sweetie, but I'm going to cut the evening short. I have things I need to do. I need to study for midterms. I'll see you tomorrow morning." He desperately hoped she wouldn't ask him to come in, because saying no was so damn hard.

Lorna told him that would be fine; she needed to study too. She said to him that she loved him and she'd see him in the morning. Phillip kissed Lorna gently on the lips, looked her in the eyes and said, "Lorna, I want you to know, there's nothing I wouldn't do for you. I love you more than I've ever loved anyone in my entire life." He kissed her once more.

Phillip got out of the car and walked her to the door. He kissed her softly in the doorway, said goodnight, and told her he was looking forward to going to Frankenmuth with her. Lorna told him she was excited about going too. She watched him go back to his car then drive away.

The Settlement

Chapter 7

Midterms were upon Phillip and Lorna. Nerves were on edge, the tension was high, and despite all that, Lorna was excited to get started on her new adventure. Each day they took one exam that was 3 to 4 hours long. Phillip walked her to class and they met each other after the exam. They'd both spent lots of time in the library, as did everyone else. They studied long hours; they helped each other a lot. Never in all the time had they known each other had they spent so much time together without touching one another.

They prepared for their chemistry project with Tammy and Scott. Wednesday came and they did their presentation. They took their exam then left together to the library. The rest of the week was the same. Friday came and Phillip had one more exam to take, then they both would be done. All the students had been notified that if they weren't going home for Thanksgiving break their grades would be available in the office Monday.

Six a.m. Saturday morning came quick. Lorna's alarm went off. Her eyes popped open and she lay there collecting her thoughts. Looking over at Connie's bed, she wondered if she was ok. Lorna had been told that when everyone resumed classes after Thanksgiving, she'd be getting a new roommate. She wasn't looking forward to it at all; they're noisy and always wanting to party, not to mention she couldn't have Phillip sneak in at night anymore!

Lorna got up, showered, and was ready in record time. She was all packed and ready to go. At 7 a.m. Phillip was out front just as promised. Lorna grabbed her overnight bag and headed out the door, so excited she could barely stand it. Walking out the door, Phillip ran up to meet her. He leaned in quickly to kiss her good morning and took her bag from her. He put her bag in the back seat of the car then hopped in. Looking over at Lorna, Phillip smiled suspiciously and said, "Are you ready for a weekend you won't ever forget?"

Lorna enthusiastically replied, "Yes, I can't wait! Let's go!" She clapped her hands together with excitement. Phillip suggested they stop for coffee and donuts before they hit the road. Lorna was all for it. Phillip drove down Dix Highway to the closest Dunkin' Donuts. They ran in and quickly got their hot coffee and donuts to go. They ate, laughed, sipped incredibly hot coffee and sang to the radio. Phillip hit the open highway heading for Saginaw, Michigan. Phillip told Lorna that it was probably about two hours away. The sun was coming up and it was a chilly morning, but Lorna didn't care as long as they were together.

Lorna saw signs that read Frankenmuth, stay right. Feeling excited, Phillip reached over and took Lorna's hand, holding it firmly. He glanced quickly at her, "I love you, Lorna. I'm so excited for this weekend." Moving his eyes from the road to Lorna, he revealed his perfect smile. Lorna returned the same charm and thought to herself, how did I get so lucky?

They finally made it to Fisher's Inn. "Oh my goodness, Phillip, it's beautiful and so big." Phillip looked at Lorna then smiled. They parked the car and went into the inn. Lorna looked all around, admiring the history. They approached the counter with Phillip stating, "Powell, here for check in."

The man behind the counter checked the book and looked up, stating, "Sir, yes I have your reservation right here. Your room is all ready for you. You're in room 12. Here's your key. Checkout is at 11 a.m. Please enjoy your stay here, and Mr. Powell?

If there's anything we can do for you to make your stay here more enjoyable, please don't hesitate to ask! Johnny will show you the way to your room."

He snapped his fingers, calling for Johnny. He looked at Johnny, "Please show Mr. Powell and his guest to their room." The bellhop bent down, grabbed their bags, and asked them to follow him.

Lorna was overwhelmed; she'd never been treated like that before. She whispered to Phillip, "Have you been here before?" Phillip said, "No. Father has though." It was apparent that everyone knew the Powell name. The bellhop took them to their room. Phillip tipped the bellhop, for which he earned a smile, and the bellhop left. Lorna stood in the middle of the room taking it all in. One big bed, a dresser, beautiful pictures of flowers on the walls, a wingback chair in the corner, and round table with two chairs by the window. There was a dressing mirror as well as a bathroom with a shower.

"It's so nice, Phillip! This is my first time being in a hotel," she said with a wry smile.

Phillip said, "Stick with me kid; I'll show you all kinds of stuff." Chuckling, he asked her, "Okay, you ready to start this day?"

"Yes, let's go!" Lorna zipped her coat up and put her gloves on.

They left the inn and started their journey down the street. There was so much to look at and everything smelled so good! It was cold and brisk outside with flurries of snow, but they didn't care. They held hands and went from shop to shop. They bought souvenirs for Lorna's family; jump ropes, Yo-Yo's, kazoos. Lorna got her sister Kitty a jewelry box with a ballerina that moved to music when you opened it. For her mother she bought a beautiful gold cross necklace and her father a silver-plated pocket watch. They spent all day walking around enjoying each others company. It was starting to get late and Phillip mentioned he was getting hungry. They went back to the inn and ate in the restaurant. They both had the chicken dinner. Lorna told Phillip it was the best chicken she'd ever tasted and laughing, she asked Phillip not to mention she'd said that to her mom. They finished their dinner and went back to their room.

Phillip put the key in and opened the door. Lorna walked in and her mouth opened in shock. With wide eyes, she gasped, put her hand over her mouth, turned to Phillip and said, "Oh my gosh, Phillip, what is all of this?" Looking at Phillip with surprise, she took in the red roses that filled the room, the petals tossed here and there over the floor and bed, and the champagne chilling on ice.

Phillip walked over to Lorna and helped her out of her coat. He laid it on a chair in the corner. He walked over to his bag, took out a small radio, and plugged it in. Once Phillip found the station he wanted, he lite two candles on the table and turned the lights off. Lorna stood watching him, wondering what he was doing. He walked over to Lorna and held his hand out. "May I have this dance?" Lorna realized the situation was about to get very serious! Lorna put her hand in Phillip's and they slow danced around the room. They kissed and held each other tight.

Phillip backed up and let go of Lorna. He stood still staring into her big eyes and could see the candlelight twinkling in them. Phillip took a deep breath, then exhaled. Tears welled up in his eyes, and he reached into his pants pocket. Taking Lorna by her left hand, he took another deep breath and knelt down on one knee. Lorna let out a gasp and covered her mouth in shock.

Phillip, leaning on one knee, exhaled and looked up at her. With a shaky, raspy voice, he began. "Lorna Jean Collins, from the day I first met you I have loved you. You changed my life forever. You showed me what love feels like. Until I loved you, Lorna, I was dead inside. You gave me something, a reason to be a better version of myself. You're my saving grace and I never want that to end. You're the most beautiful, humble, confident, strong, amazing woman I've ever known in my life!

When I look into your eye's, Lorna, I see my future. You're my best friend. You're whom I am to grow old with. You are my soul mate.

I know that I hurt you and given the chance I will spend the rest of my life showing you how sorry I am. I promised myself that if God ever gave you back to me, I'd never let you go again. I promise to love you forever, every single day of my life. Lorna, will you please do me the honor of growing old with me. I believe the best is yet to come. I promise you, Lorna, no one will work harder to make you happy or cherish you more than me. So, Lorna, will you please do me the honor of marrying me?" The tears fell from Phillip's eyes as he waited for Lorna's answer.

Lorna took her hand from her mouth and as the tears streamed down her face, she cried, "YES! Oh my gosh, yes! Yes, Phillip, I will marry you!" She let out a squeal of excitement as she watched Phillip slid a diamond ring onto her shaky left ring finger. Phillip stood while Lorna held up her hand to view the ring. She realized it was the same one she picked out at the jewelry store.

She looked up at Phillip, "This is the same ring I had on! How'd you get this?" She stared at him with her tear-soaked eyes.

Phillip said, "After I cut our night short, I went right back to the jewelry store and purchased this ring. I had to get it; I saw how your face lite up when you put it on. Lorna, this was the whole purpose for this weekend. I'm just so grateful it went the way I'd planned...or that would've been an awkward ride home," he laughed out loud. His smile was triumphant as he blinked, his gaze serious and eyelashes wet, while he stared into Lorna's eyes.

"Oh, Phillip! It's beautiful! Absolutely beautiful! I love it so much. Thank you! Thank you for asking me to be your wife! I can't believe this is even happening.....I feel like this is a fairytale or a dream that I'm going to wake up from," she told him, sounding almost pitiful.

"Lorna, I can assure you that this isn't a dream. But you were right about the fairytale, because you're my princess." Leaning in, he kissed her softly on the lips. He moved away from her and over to the table. He took the bottle of champagne out of the chilled bucket, peeled the foil from it, twisted the metal wire away, and pushed up on the plastic cork. It made a loud "pop" and smoke floated out of the top making them both laugh. Phillip filled the champagne glasses, turned to Lorna and handed her a glass. Raising his glass to hers, he said, "Here's to us, to the rest of our lives together, and to you, the future Mrs. Phillip Powell." Lorna had a sober look come across her face.

Phillip looked puzzled, asking, "Is everything ok?"

"Don't be silly. Everything is perfect," she told him as she reflected on the arrangement she made with Mr. Powell and how she still hadn't told Phillip. She still didn't know how he would take the news. She focused back on Phillip, reassuring him that everything was fine, and took a sip of her champagne. She made a funny face, then swallowed.

"It tickles my nose," she said, rubbing her hand across the end of her nose. "Would you be hurt if I told you this tastes terrible?"

"Honestly, Lorna, I don't think anyone likes champagne. How could they? It smells like rotten eggs." They both broke into laughter again.

Phillip set their glasses down and made his way over to Lorna. The radio was still on. He lifted his hand up to her face and cupped the nape of her neck. He laid his right hand on her hip and twirled her around in circles, dancing across the floor. Lorna started slowly undressing him, dropping his clothes to the floor. She led him to the bed and slowly laid him down. He slid himself up on the bed, not removing his gaze from her eyes, so full of lust and desire. Lorna stood in front of him, slowly starting to take her clothes off. She dropped one piece at a time to the floor. Fully aroused, Phillip laid on the bed watching her. Lorna was standing in front of Phillip completely naked. She stood,

twisting her long blonde hair, biting her bottom lip.
Phillip found that so erotic he could hardly stand it.
He beckoned Lorna to move onto the bed.

Lorna started kissing Phillip feet first, working her
way up to his thighs and then between his legs.

Running her tongue across his erect manhood, she
took her hand and gently wrapped her hands
around his girth moving her hand up and down.

Phillip closed his eyes and let out a moan. Lorna
handled his girth like a lollipop, licking gently, her
warm breath and wet saliva tantalizing. She lightly
grazed him with her teeth, swirling her tongue
around the top, making him lose all sense and
control as she softly moved up and down. Rubbing
her hands all over him, she engulfed him in her
mouth. Phillip groaned and his eyes flickered open.
He lifted his head to watch and almost lost himself
right there. He grabbed the back of her head,
wound his fingers through her hair, and started
moving her head up and down on him, thrusting in
and out of her mouth.

Lorna pulled him out of her mouth and traveled
her way up to his navel, bathing him with her
tongue and placing feather-light kisses all over his
perfect chest. She moved up to his lips, lowered
herself down, and placed her full weight on top of
him. Phillip slid his hands around her face and
kissed her long and hard. Seductively, as their
tongues explored each other's intimate arousal, their

bodies responded to the want of each other. Phillip sat up and turned, dropping Lorna down on the bed. He held her face in his hands as he laid half on and half off her. He cupped her breast in his hand, gently licking and nibbling on her erect nipples. He kissed up and down on her face and neck, rubbing her whole body. He slid his hand slowly down the full length of her torso and down between her legs, cupping her aching body in his hand. He rubbed slowly, sliding his middle finger inside of her.

Lorna moaned, arching her back, and voluntarily opened her legs as Phillip moved his hand slowly in and out of her. Lorna reached over, grasped him again in her hand and began moving it in rhythm with Phillip.

Lorna halted her rhythm, making Phillip slow his, and she gently laid him on his back. She straddled him, placing his girth back in her hand and guided him inside of her. She slowly slid down to the base of him and then back up again. Phillip reached for her to caress both breasts as Lorna arched her back. With her head thrown back, she closed her eyes and let her long hair cascade down her back. She thrust her hips back and forth, faster, faster, feeling the sensation building inside her. She felt her blood burning with erotic emotion and the pressure built inside her and finally took over as she lost all sense of control and exploded inside. When Phillip knew Lorna had finished, he sat up suddenly and got on his knees. He flipped her over on her knees, spread her legs apart, and placed his hand on the small of her back. Phillip pressed firmly with his hand, forcing her to arch her back. Phillip entered her from behind. He held her hips, thrusting faster and faster until he emptied himself inside of her.

Completely breathless, he dropped down onto Lorna's backside. Wrapping his arm around her waist, he hugged tightly.

Kissing her back, he said in a breathy tone, "Whew! That was incredible! Holy shit, where'd that come from?" He laid his head on her back.

Lorna chuckled, "I don't know, I listen to people when they talk."

"Well if I were your daddy, I'd be telling you to find new friends. But since it was used on me, all I can say is...Whoa!!!" Lorna laughed out loud.

Phillip let go of her, and they got up. They put on their nightclothes, blew out the candles, brushed their teeth together and got into bed. Lorna laid there snuggled into Phillip, nice and warm, feeling her ring on her finger. With a big smile on her face, she said, "I love you, Phillip. Thank you again for asking me to marry you."

"Thank you for saying yes...I love you, too, my future bride!" Lorna smiled big as Phillip snuggled into her tighter. They both fell asleep in each other's arms.

The sun was shining through a crack in the window curtain. Phillip lifted his head to see the time. He looked down at Lorna, still sound asleep. Phillip laid there watching Lorna as she slept, remembering the entire night, from the proposal to making love. What a fantastic night it was! He knew it wasn't something he'd forget anytime soon. He lifted his hand and lightly lifted a few strands of hair from Lorna's face. She moved a little, opened her eyes, and saw Phillip looking down at her.

She stretched and gave a little yawn. "Good morning, handsome. Ya know, a gal could get used to waking up to someone as good looking as you."

He said, "I sure hope so. I think you might be stuck with me," he told her with a smile.

Lorna threw her left hand up in the air as though she'd forgot that Phillip had proposed. She stared at her ring with a whimsical smile on her face saying, "Mrs. Lorna Powell. Mrs. Powell. Mr. and Mrs. Dr. Phillip Powell. Oh, I love the sound of that. I'm getting married. Holy cow! I can't believe I'm marrying Phillip Powell!" She let out a giggle as she snuggled into Phillip.

They laid there for a few minutes enjoying the morning. It was almost 8 o'clock and Phillip reminded her they had to check out by 11. He decided to go get them coffee and something to eat.

He jumped out of bed, got dressed, and ran into the bathroom where Lorna could hear him brushing his teeth. He finished and told her he'd be right back.

Lorna got up, grabbed her cosmetic bag, and headed for the bathroom. She brushed her teeth and turned on the shower. She dropped her robe, stepped into the warm shower, and closed her eyes while water cascaded down her body. She stood there transfixed by the warmth of the warm water and Phillips proposal. I'm engaged to Phillip Powell, she thought. Suddenly, she felt someone touch her. Quickly she opened her eyes and put her hand over her heart. "Phillip! You scared the dickens out of me." He put his finger on her lips and moved in closer to her. Moving his hand slowly away, he pressed his lips to hers. He reached over, grabbed a bar of soap and with his hand slid it up and down her beautiful wet body.

As the water splashed down on their faces, they ran their hands all over each other's bodies. Phillip took the soap and ran it up to her breast, slowly running it over her erect nipples. He lathered soap all over Lorna's young, hard body. He dropped the soap to the floor and with his soapy hands he ran them up and down her warm wet skin. Lorna tilted her head back under the water, closing her eyes, letting the sensual water run down her face while Phillip pleasured her in such an erotic way. He was more aggressive than the night before, but she didn't care. The feeling was stimulating, alluring, and she squirmed in pleasure. Her desire for Phillip to be inside of her was getting harder to resist. Phillip's voice was soft as he grabbed her wet hair and kissed her on the lips. She was mesmerized. He swept over her lips with his tongue, and nibbled her lower lip lightly and seductively. He gnawed at her chin, gliding his teeth down her neck down to her collarbone, kissing and sucking on her neck.

Phillip slid his hand down between her legs, running his hand lightly across her. Teasing her to the point Lorna was moaning and almost begging him to enter her. Breathing heavy, Lorna told him with a heavy tone that she wanted him inside of her. He moved to her mouth again, kissing her hard, running his hands up to her breasts. He took her nipples between his fingers, squeezing gently and massaging them. Her body was like a soldier at full attention and electricity shot straight through her body. It was so erotic that her body was burning for him to touch her inner self.

Lorna slightly opened her eyes and with a rapidly pounding heart looked at Phillip. She opened her mouth slightly to help with her breathing. She slid her hand down to Phillip's full manhood. Moving her hand back and forth, sliding her hand between his legs, she massaged him gently in her hand. Lorna lifted one leg, coiling it around Phillip's strong, hard body, and took his girth in her hand to guide it inside of her. Phillip held on to her as she gasped in pleasure and fell against the shower wall. Phillip thrust in and out of her as Lorna held onto Phillip's backside. As the warm water fell between them, Lorna lost all sense of her being. Her body went hot inside and as she reached her peak she let herself go with an explosion that made her body shake. Phillip held on tight and moved in and out a few more times before he emptied inside of her.

Lorna dropped her tired arms down to Phillip's shoulders, laid her head on him, and with pounding hearts they both exclaimed with labored breath, "Wow, holy crap!"

They finished their showers, got dressed, checked out of the inn, and headed home. Lorna stared at her ring almost the entire way back to school, telling Phillip how much she loved her ring and him. They talked all the way home, discussing when they'd like to get married. They talked about school as well. Both were curious about their grades, which would be available on Monday. They stopped at a McDonald's for lunch and headed back to school.

The Settlement

Chapter 8

Lorna knew that her college experience was a rite of passage and she felt the need to excel. After all, it was her lifelong dream. Monday morning already and it was time to find out if she was smart enough to stay at the University of Michigan. The first time playing in the big league was a little unsettling for her. Even though she knew that her grades from midterms wouldn't appear on her transcript, nor be calculated into her GPA, she still wanted to know how she was doing. Rolling over to look at the alarm, she had a couple of minutes before Showtime. Reaching up to turn it off, her ring sparked in the light. A big smile flickered across her face as she relished the moment and her engagement to Phillip Powell.

Lorna sat up on the edge of her bed, grabbed her stuff and headed to the shower. An hour later, she met Phillip in the cafeteria for breakfast. Lorna saw

Phillip sitting in the cafeteria by the window looking out staring at nothing. She went in, walked over to him, and touched his shoulder. He jumped a little, as though she'd startled him. Phillip looked up at her smiling and stood up.

He kissed her saying, "Good morning...fiancé," with a charming smile.
Lorna smiled wide and dropped her head down, swaying back and forth while twisting her hair and biting her bottom lip. They ate breakfast and left the cafeteria hand in hand, heading to the main building to get their grades and then to spend the whole day together doing nothing. They walked in the office separately, with Lorna going first. She saw her grades; straight A's all the way down. She was handed an envelope. She came rushing out of the office with a smile the size of New York yelling, "I did it, Phillip! I did it!" She threw her arms around his neck and kissed him. "Now, your turn Dr. Powell." Phillip chuckled, then walked through the doors. He, too, viewed his grades. All A's except one B+. He was very pleased. The receptionist handed him a letter as well. He walked out to see Lorna reading her letter. She looked up at Phillip and asked him about his grades. He told her and then said, "You got a letter too?"

"Yes, it says that Dean Evans wants to speak with me as soon as possible."

Phillip, too, opened his letter and it said the same thing. "Umm, I wonder what this is all about?" He looked puzzled and had his eyebrows pushed together.

"I don't know, but let's go find out," Lorna expressed eagerly. She jumped up, grabbing Phillips arm, and practically pulled him down the hall. The dean's office was down the hall from the main office. They rapped on his door and heard a voice say, "Come on in." Phillip opened the door and they went in together. "Oh, you're both here...together!" the dean said, sitting up in his chair. "Phillip, I'd like to speak to you both separately if you don't mind?"

"No, not at all," Phillip said, and started to walk out of the room.

"Phillip wait. I'd like to speak to you first. Lorna, if you don't mind, have a seat in the waiting area and please shut the door on your way out," replied the dean with a stern face.

"Please, have a seat," the dean said, waving his hand in the direction of a chair. Phillip sat down, looked at the dean, then said, "Sir, what's this all about?"

"Phillip, I have your transcript in front of me. I feel so bad that I have to do this to you. Phillip, you're a brilliant young man with an auspicious future ahead of you, but as you very well know, medical school is very expensive. You have an outstanding bill in a rather large amount. I hate to say this, but if you can't pay for your tuition then, son, I'm going to have to ask you to leave." The dean rested his elbows on his desk while folding his fingers together.

Phillip sat there in shock. His head started to spin with unclear thoughts. Narrowing his eyebrows, Phillip replied, "I'm sorry, didn't my father already pay for my tuition for this semester?"

"No. I don't see anything in the records proving that statement to be true."
Phillip was becoming irritated and feeling enraged and demanded that the dean look again. "I'm sorry Phillip, I've looked twice now. Maybe you should get a hold of your father and see what happened. It's probably a misunderstanding that can be cleared up with one phone call." The dean leaned back in his chair, looking smug and arrogant. Phillip thought, that's the keyword, "father!" He found out about Lorna and me and now he's cut me off. I'm in breach of my contract with him. Now I have to leave school. Phillip stood up, reached across the desk and extended his hand to

Dean Evans. They shook hands and Phillip told him he'd take care of it.

Dean Evans said, "I sure hope so, Phillip. You have a brilliant mind and it would be a shame to let that go to waste. You're going to make a find doctor someday. Hope to see you back here soon. Good luck son," he said with a smug smile on his face. "Oh, and Phillip, could you please send in Miss Collins."

Phillip walked through the door looking like someone had just punched him in the guts. Lorna looked up at him. Seeing the devastated look on his face, she said, "Oh my goodness are you ok? What happened?"

Phillip said, "I'll tell you in a few minutes. He wants to see you now." He dropped his head, downcast.

Lorna slowly got up and walked to the door. She rapped lightly. From behind the door, she heard the dean say, "Come in." She opened the door and walked to the center of the room. He motioned for her to sit down. Lorna sat down on the edge of the chair and looked at the dean.

Dean Evans sat straight up, cleared his throat and looked at Lorna. "Well, Lorna, this puts me in an awkward position. Looking at your transcript, I can see you're a brilliant young lady. You graduated class valedictorian with the highest honors, which makes this very difficult for me to have to tell you this." Clearing his throat again and collapsing his hands together on his lap, he said, "Lorna, I truly regret to have to tell you this, but I have to ask you to clear out your room. Your presence is no longer welcome at this school," he told her with a sober tone.

"What? This has got to be a mistake. Why? I don't…," she broke off, her thoughts turning to the arrangement she'd made with Theodore Powell. Lorna's heart sank when she realized what this was all about. Tears formed in her eyes as her stomach flipped. She stood up and said, "I understand. I'm sorry it came to this. How long do I have to get my stuff out?"

"Immediately. No exceptions!" the dean told her, returning his eyes to the folders laying on his desk.

Lorna wiped the tears from her face and walked toward the door. Opening the door, Phillip stood up, saw Lorna was crying, and looking puzzled he said, "What's wrong? Why are you crying?" Lorna said in a pitiful voice, "C'mon let's go, Phillip. We need to talk. There's something I need to tell you."

Phillip reached out, took Lorna's hand, and held it tight as they walked out together. It was starting to snow. With the cold wind blowing in their faces, Lorna looked up at the sky and watched the snow fall as it landed on her tear-soaked face. Her head was spinning. Her thoughts were out of control. The more she thought about it, the angrier she became. Phillip was burning inside, thinking to himself that his father must have found out about him and Lorna. As his anger grew inside of him, Lorna suggested they sit in Phillip's car so they'd have some privacy. They walked over to his car and got in. Phillip started the car to warm it up and they both sat there in silence for a few minutes collecting their thoughts.

They sat in the car looking at each other until Phillip suggested that Lorna go first. She insisted that he go first as the knots got tighter in her stomach. Phillip put his hand on hers and told her that his father must know about them. He told her he had been completely cut off from the family money. Now he had a huge outstanding bill from the school and unless full payment was immediately taken care of he couldn't continue his studies at U of M. He told her that it didn't matter to him for as long as he had her everything would be ok.

Lorna looked at Phillip with tears in her eyes, saying in a soft tone, "Oh, Phillip, I'm so sorry. Me coming to this school has ruined your chance of becoming a doctor." The tears ran freely down her cheeks.

Phillip took his thumb, wiped the tears from her face, and assured her that he'd rather have her. He loved her and couldn't wait to marry her, despite what his father thought. Then he said, "Now tell me what's wrong with you? Why'd the dean want to talk to you?"

Lorna took a deep breath, exhaled, and looked Phillip directly in the eyes. She said, "What I have to tell you isn't going to be easy for you to hear. Phillip, haven't you wondered how it was possible for me to come to this school?" The tears fell from her eyes as she put her hand on his and looked back up at him. "Phillip, when I was living in your house, I learned a few things and your father bought my silence with an arrangement I signed with him." Phillip quickly pulled his hand from hers, moving away. His eyes narrowed and grew cold. With his eyebrows pushed together, he said, "What the hell are you talking about?" in a rough voice.

Lorna drew her hands close to her stomach, noticing Phillip's rage. It was unsettling and she said, "While I lived in your house I overheard your father and Dr. Kendal talking in his study. I heard that your father was keeping your mother medicated for no reason at all! Phillip, there is nothing wrong with your mother. Your dad keeps her medicated, over medicated at certain times because …. Oh my gosh, Phillip, I'm so sorry to have to tell you this, but your father is raping Lois. I witnessed him coming out of her room in the middle of the night. He knew I saw him and there was no denying it. I head Dr. Kendal begging him to stop medicating your mom and he refused. They got in a big fight and your father threatened the doctor. Your father vowed to destroy him if he opened his mouth, but then I confronted him. To make a long story short, he had his lawyers write up an arrangement that I signed. He bought my silence with a check on my 18th birthday for $100,000. The arrangement was that I was never to contact you or ever talk to you again or he would blackball me from all colleges in the state of Michigan. Well, he obviously knows about you and me because the dean told me that I have to leave the school at once." Her voice was shaky as tears fell from her eyes and she watched the color drain from Phillip's face.

Phillip blinked back tears as he looked out the window of his car. He then focused his attention again on Lorna. He said, "Who the fuck are you? I don't even know you. You've known all this time about that and NOT once did you try to tell me. Lois is like a sister to me. I love those two girls and my father is raping her! And you have done NOTHING about it. Instead, you sold your soul to the devil, took the money and ran! You disgust me, Lorna! Get out of my car!" His voice was hoarse and Lorna hardly recognized it.

"Wait, Phillip, let me explain. Part of the arrangement that your father signed was that he was never to touch Lois again and the last I checked he hadn't touched her."

"Do you have any idea who you're fucking with? He's Satan himself! You don't ride the train for free, Lorna, and you can't get on the bus with half a ticket. My father is not one to reckon with. He is ruthless and ALWAYS gets what he wants, no matter who he hurts, and what about my mother? Did you think of how medicated my mother has been since my brother died? My mother has been trapped in her own body because of my father and AGAIN you did nothing. Lorna, get out of my car! I honestly can't look at you anymore!"

"Phillip, please, can we talk about this? I did try to tell you! Every time I tried, we were always interrupted and then the moment was gone. But in retrospect, Phillip, you did the same thing to me. You left me for your father's money!"

Phillip said, "Are you seriously trying to make what I did to you the same as what you did? I'm not splitting hairs with you about this. You're not going to get me to see both sides of the coin. What you did was wrong and you're as guilty as my father for not saying anything to anyone about what he was doing. If you think I'm indignant, then look in the mirror, Lorna! What you'll see staring back at you is my father! Phillip reached over the top of

Lorna's lap to the door handle, pulling on it the door and forcefully pushing it open.

He looked at Lorna with rage in his eyes and said, "For the last time, Lorna, GET THE FUCK OUT OF MY CAR!" He sat there enraged, his jaws clenched together.

Lorna, crying hysterically, turned in her seat, put her feet on the cement and turned to look back at Phillip. He turned his head away so he didn't have to look at her. Lorna said, "Phillip, I'm so sorry. I did try to tell you a couple of times."

"Well, obviously you didn't try hard enough, now did you?" he told her, staring out the window.

"Phillip, I love you!" Lorna said with desperation in her voice.

Phillip never uttered a single word. Lorna closed the car door and backed away from the car. Phillip took off in a rage, squealing his tires, laying rubber on the cement and leaving a cloud of smoke behind him. Lorna watched the love of her life drive off in a rage. Lorna had never seen Phillip so angry and she wasn't sure if he would ever forgive her or ever come back to her again.

The Settlement

Chapter 9

Lorna went back to her dorm room. She stood in the middle of the room looking around, knowing that she had to leave college, and this would change the trajectory of her life. Becoming a pediatrician was something she'd dreamed of her whole life. Phillip's anger at Lorna made her heart hurt so bad that it felt utterly broken. She stood there thinking if she'd just thrown caution to the wind, risked it all, and told Phillip a while ago, then maybe this wouldn't have happened. Oh God, was Phillip right? Was she no different than his father? No different than a man she thoroughly despised? How'd she get so caught up in coming to this college and his money?

She thought of a verse from the Bible, 1 Timothy 6:10: 'For the love of money is a root of all kinds of evil. Some people, eager for money, have wandered from the faith and pierced themselves with many griefs.' Lorna wrapped her arms around her waist and fell to the floor. She cried hysterically, to the point she could barely breathe.

Getting to her knees, she put her hands together and prayed to God, asking for his forgiveness. She never realized what she'd become and how she was no different than Theodore Powell.

Lorna pulled herself together, then started to pack up her room. Everything went back into the boxes she'd brought it in. Tears rolled down her face while putting her books into a box. It was as though she was closing a chapter on her new life, one that she wasn't ready to say goodbye to. She stacked the boxes up in the middle of her room. She was tired. Her eyes were stinging from crying and she was mentally exhausted from her emotional day. She went over to her bed, thinking I'll call my dad in a little while to come get me tomorrow. She closed her eyes thinking about Phillip, wondering where he was and if she'd ever see him again.

Lorna woke to a tap on her door. It took her a few minutes to realize someone was rapping on her door. She hopped out of bed and moved quickly toward the door. She opened it and there he was, standing in the doorway.

Lorna was so happy to see him she ran right to him, throwing her arms around him. Phillip barely touched her. He put his hands on her shoulders and pushed her off him. Lorna stepped back and quietly looked up at him.

Phillip, looking at Lorna, said, "I'm not ready for that yet. I need some answers," he told her with a soft, sad tone in his voice.

"Sure, I understand. Do you want to come in for a minute?"

"Sure, for a minute."

Lorna's heart broke. He walked in and saw the pile of boxes in the middle of the room and realized she was leaving. He asked, "Who's coming to get you? And when are you leaving?"

Lorna, while sitting down on the edge of her bed, said, "I'm calling my dad in the morning. I didn't call home yet. I wasn't in the mood to fake a happy me when I'd be lying. My dad can always tell when I'm not truthful."

"Umm, maybe I better ask him what the secret is!" he said sarcastically.

"Did you come to hurt me more or do you want some answers?" Looking downcast, she swirled her socked foot on the hardwood floor.

Phillip stood in the middle of the room with his hands in his pockets looking at Lorna's beautiful, sad face. The pain she was feeling was written all over it. Although it was killing Phillip to see her so upset, he wasn't ready to forget and forgive, being still angry and confused.

"Ok," Phillip said, "Tell me again the whole story about what you saw and heard. I need to hear it again." He walked over to the other empty bed, sat down, took off his jacket, and looked over at Lorna.

Lorna started from the beginning and then rehashed the entire story again, tears streaming down her face. Phillip said, "Does Lois know you know about what my father is doing?"

"Yes, Phillip. Honestly, I tried talking her into turning him in. She boldly told me to stay out of it and that it was none of my business. Everyone in that house knows their place and if she said anything they'd all be thrown out on the street. She said none of them had anywhere else to go. So I was told to shut my mouth and stay out of it."

"So she's letting my father do that to her because she's in fear of not having anywhere to live. That's fucking sad and it breaks my heart. My father knows that, too, and that's why he's doing it to her. Now what about my mother? How'd she seem to you?"

"Your mom and I got to be very close when I was there. Your mom is a beautiful woman inside and out. I let her feel the baby kicking. We laughed and talked all the time, but only when your father was away, though. When he was gone, your mother wouldn't take her medicine. She told me all the time how good she'd felt when she went without her medicine. Then your father would come home and force feed it to her again. Phillip, I feel so sorry for your mom. It's so sad." Lorna looked up at Phillip and the tears were running down his face.

Phillip, while wiping the tears from his face, said, "There's so much sadness in my house. It has been like that for many years."

"Phillip, your house is cold, dark, and full of evil," Lorna said with her eyebrows pushed together.

"You're so right, Lorna, and it needs to change right now!" Phillip said. He got to his feet and with his hands waving in the air he told her, "I'm so fucking done! I can't do this with Father any more. I'm going home to take care of this shit and make everyone's life better, including ours."

Lorna's face lite up as a big smile crossed her lips, "Ours? You mean you and I together?"

"Of course, silly. I was angry at Father and hurt you didn't tell me sooner what was going on behind closed doors at my own house. Lorna, I still love you just as much as I always did. It was just a lot for me to take in. Now both of us have to leave school and then what?"

"I don't know yet. We'll figure it out. As long as we're together, we can conquer anything."
Phillip walked across the room and over to Lorna.
He knelt down on his knees in front of her, wrapped his arms around her and hugged her tight.

He backed his head up, staring into her tired blue eyes and said, "I love you so much Lorna! That will never change. I'm so sorry for talking to you the way I did. I promise I won't ever do that again. I hope you can find it in your
heart to forgive me for being such a jerk. Even if I can't come back to this school or ever become a doctor, having all of that and not having you isn't worth it to me. I am going to marry you and the rest will work itself out. I'm exhausted. We need to get some sleep because you and I are going home tomorrow."

Lorna's eyes got big and she said to him with excitement in her voice, "Really? We're going home...together?"

"Yes, of course. What else can my father do to us?"
Lorna hugged him tight. They curled into bed and snuggled together, saying goodbye to an awful day they didn't care to remember.

Morning came and found them both up and ready to go. They loaded the car with all of their belongings. As they pulled away from the school Lorna's heart broke. Her eyes filled with tears as she had to say goodbye to her dream. Phillip stopped for coffee and donuts and they pulled onto M-23 heading east as they headed back home to Yale, Michigan. It was a bittersweet moment for the both of them. They were excited to go back home to see everyone, but not under these circumstances.

Lorna wasn't sure how to explain any of this to her parents. She wasn't just embarrassed, she was ashamed and scared to death to tell her dad that she and Phillip were not only back together but they were also engaged to be married. Phillip sat quietly glancing at Lorna from time to time, giving her a wry smile. Phillip's concern wasn't on school or Lorna's parents; his focus was solely on his father and what he'd been doing to Lois and his mother. The rage was burning deep inside of him until it almost consumed him.

Lorna reached over to take Phillip's hand, telling him she loved him, and asking if he was ok. Phillip told her he was ok and that he'd be even better when he saw that his mother and Lois were ok.

Phillip said, "One more question. Does Minnie know what father is doing to Lois?"

"Gosh, I don't think so. Honestly, I don't think anyone does, other than me of course."
Phillip reached up, rubbed his perfectly chiseled jaw, and murmured, "Umm" while staring out the window at the open road. Phillip sat straight in his seat and settled in for the long ride ahead. The more he thought of what his father was doing, the faster he drove. Lorna had to tell him a couple of times to slow down, that he was going to fast. All

of a sudden, Phillip looked up in his rearview mirror and said, "Shit," as he slowed the car.

Lorna quickly turned to look behind her saying, "Oh no," and turned back to Phillip.

Phillip pulled the car off to the side of the highway, parked the car and waited. The police car pulled up behind them and the officer got out, walking to the driver's side. Phillip rolled his window down.

Phillip said, "Morning officer. What can I do for you?"

"Sir, do you know how fast you were going?"

"No, honestly, I don't."

"I clocked you doing 12 over the posted speed limit. Sir, I need to see your license and registration." The officer stood in the cold wind with his pad in hand, ready to deliver a ticket to Phillip.

Phillip reached into the glove box retrieving his registration. He lifted himself up, pulled his wallet from the back pocket of his pants, opened it and pulled out his license. He then handed both to the officer.

The officer said, "I'll be right back" and walked to his car.

Phillip sat waiting and Lorna didn't say a word. They sat in silence waiting for the officer to come back to the car. A few minutes later, Phillip looked in his side mirror and saw the officer coming back.

Phillip rolled the window down again and the officer handed him back his license and registration.

The officer looked down at Phillip and said, "Mr. Powell, you need to slow down and be more careful." He turned, walking away.

Phillip instantly got mad. He poked his head out the car window and said, "Excuse me, are you telling me that you're not given me a ticket?"

The officer stopped on a dime, pivoted on one heel turning sideways and said, "Yes, Mr. Powell, that's what I'm saying. You can leave Mr. Powell. I recommend you slow down."

"I'm sorry, but that's not acceptable to me. I noticed you keep calling Mr. Powell. Yes, I'm Theodore Powell's son, but I don't want any special treatment because of that. My father has bullied and pushed around so many people and everyone is so afraid of him, but it stops here. Officer, if I was anyone else would I have gotten a ticket today?"

The officer cleared his throat, adjusted his hat, then said, "Well, I'm letting you off with a warning. Just be happy with that and get on your way before I change my mind."

"Please do change your mind. I was speeding and I broke the law. Just because I'm a Powell doesn't make me above the law. So please do change your mind--I deserve a ticket just like anyone else."

"I'm sorry, are you seriously asking me to give you a ticket?"

"Yes, precisely. Treat me like anyone else that just broke the law."

"Okay then, I'm going to need your license and registration back."

The officer went back to his car and returned a few minutes later. He handed Phillip his stuff back once again, only this time there was a ticket with it.

Phillip looked down at it, then looked up at the officer, and with a smile on his face said, "Thank you and have a nice day!"

The officer put out his hand to shake Phillip's and told him "In all my years on the force I've never witnessed anything like this before. Mr. Powell. Excuse me, Phillip that was an honorable thing you just displayed. Thank you from all the officers on the force. You have a nice day and drive safe!"

Phillip rolled up the window, put the car in drive, and pulled out onto the freeway again. Lorna looked over at him puzzled, then asked, "Are you ok?"

"Yes, Lorna my love. I'm just fine. I'm taking down my father and this horrible dark cloud that hangs over the Powell name. Everyone fears father.....well not anymore! Things are going to change and I'm going to be the one to do it." He let out a squeal of excitement while banging on the steering wheel with his hands.

The whole atmosphere changed in the car. Phillip and Lorna talked all the way home. Phillip clued her in on how he was taking control of the Powell name and how he was going to relieve the town of Yale from the horror they've lived in for many years. Things were going to change. Things had to change! Phillip drove with a wicked grin on his face halfway home. Lorna had a sinking feeling she couldn't shake that they were heading down the same old rabbit hole.

The Settlement

Chapter 10

Phillip and Lorna drove for a couple of hours, getting closer and closer to their hometown of Yale, Michigan. Everything was starting to look very familiar to them. Phillip had commented that it was so lovely to be back home and that he'd missed it. He couldn't wait to see his mother again. Lorna was excited and nervous at the same time. They both saw the sign at the same time, Yale city limits! Turning their heads toward each other, they smiled.

Phillip slowed the car down and drove slowly through town. Everything looked exactly the same as it was when he left. He pulled up in front of his house and they sat there for a few minutes just staring at it. Lorna was sick to her stomach just thinking of everything that happened while she lived there. She could still see Theodore sneaking out of Lois' room in the middle of the night adjusting his pants. How he let her whole family thinks he was such a nice guy when he gave her that big check on her 18th birthday. She thought of the arrangement they'd made. Her stomach did somersaults and she wanted to throw up. Phillip was thinking of his whole childhood growing up in that house. How for his whole life his father always treated him like a mistake, right into adulthood, and nothing he ever did was good enough for his father. His father couldn't care less that Phillip carried all A's through school and was always on the honor roll. No one mattered to his father but James. James could do no wrong in Father's eyes. Phillip remembered his sister Lily was Father's princess and got away with everything, but she still didn't have that bond that he had with James.

Phillip remembered his father always yelling and screaming at him, telling him he was nothing but trouble, "Why can't you be more like your brother James?" he'd say to him. Just at that moment, Phillip had that feeling in his heart all over again of the hurt and what a disappointment he was to his father. He remembered some good times too, though, when his father would take James away for a couple of days or longer sometimes. He, his mother, and Lily would play Pick up Sticks, jacks, cards, hide-and-seek, and I spy. They made snowmen after a big blizzard and caught lightning bugs on hot summer nights. When Lois and Vera came to live with them it added all the more fun to the house. Phillip loved his mother and those girls, and he was there to fix all the wrong that had been going on in that house. Up until Phillip met Lorna, his whole life hurt, but not anymore. He was going to release everyone from the hell of the prison his father was keeping them in.

Phillip let out a big sigh, then reached over and took Lorna by the hand saying, "You ready to do this?" with a stern face.

Lorna looked up at Phillip. "I can do anything with you by my side," she said with a wry smile.

"Ok then, let's do this!" He lifted his hand from Lorna's. After pulling the car into the drive, he stopped at the gates, got out, opened them and drove all the way to the back of the house. He turned the engine off, took in a deep breath and exhaled, deliberating. He opened the car door and Lorna followed his lead. Phillip walked around to meet Lorna, took her by the hand, and together they walked up to the back deck. Making their way to the back door, they opened it, and the aroma of Minnie's home-cooked food slapped them in the face. Phillip knew then that he was home.

Every head in the kitchen turned to see who was coming through the door. After a short pause, all you could hear were shrieking sounds of everyone's excitement. Minnie, Lois, Vera, and Richard were all in the kitchen. They dropped everything they were doing to rush over to them. They grabbed Phillip and Lorna and started hugging them.

Minnie started to cry with tears of joy. Lois came over to Phillip to throw her arms around him, hugging him as tight as she could, exclaiming "Phillip! You're home! Your really home!" With tears running down her face, Phillip held tightly to Lois, hugged and kissed her cheek and said, "Yes, Sis, I'm home!" Lois smiled wide with a sparkle in her big brown eyes.

Minnie backed up to look at both of them. With her hands resting on her hips she declared, "Lord, child, you both need to eat! You're both as thin as rails." Walking over to Lorna, she put her arms around her in a big Minnie hug and cried, "Welcome home, Sugar!"

Richard came over to Phillip and extended his hand. Phillip took his hand and pulled Richard close to him and hugged him. After Lorna had her turn, Richard said, "Welcome home you two! What brings you both home together?" he asked with a puzzled look on his face.

Phillip said, "Well, we have good news, and we came to take care of some business."

Lois blurted out…"What's the good news?" Her eyes were wide and full of excitement.
Phillip reached down, grabbed Lorna's hand and lifted it up, revealing her diamond ring. "Lorna and

I are getting married," he informed them, as a big smile flickered across both of their faces.

Minnie reached over to take Lorna's hand saying, "Oh Child...look at the size of that diamond." She moved Lorna's hand in the sunlight watching the diamond sparkle, then the girls walked in to see its brilliance. They all hugged again saying congratulations. The kitchen was a loud buzz of love and laughter. Lorna, and Phillip looked at each other with big smiles on their faces, each loving the fact that they were home and home together.

Minnie ask if they were hungry. She'd just made lunch and there was plenty for everyone. Phillip said, "Yes, but first, where is my father?"

Minnie said, "As luck would have it, he's out of town on business for a couple of days."

Phillip could feel the weight of the world lift off his shoulders and he let out a big sigh. "Where is my mother?"

"Upstairs, honey, where she always is," Minnie said with a sober tone.

Phillip said, "That's all about to change. Mother is coming down for lunch so set her a place at the table."

Phillip took Lorna by the hand. "Let's go see Mother and give her the good news," he said, walking through the kitchen. Phillip stopped at his father's study. Phillip and Lorna looked at each other but continued to the stairs. Making their way up to his mother's room, they stopped at her door before tapping. Phillip stood looking in at his mother sitting alone in the wingback chair in the corner of her room reading *Go Tell it on the Mountain* by *James Baldwin.* She looked so frail and older than Phillip remembered, but she looked angelic and at peace.

Phillip lifted his hand and lightly tapped on the frame of her door. Looking up from her book, she went to speak and nothing came out. Audrey had such a look of surprise on her face that she instantly began to cry. Setting her book down on the stand next to her, she rose from her chair slowly and moved toward the center of the room with her arms extended outward, waiting for Phillip to fill them.

Phillip hurried to his mother and into her waiting arms. She embraced him so tightly he could barely breathe. Audrey kissed her son on the cheek a few times, backed up to look him in the eyes and said, "Son, you're finally home." She held him with tears streaming down her face.

"Yes, Mother, I'm home. And look who I brought with me," he said, turning to look at Lorna.

Audrey opened her arms for Lorna and embraced her. Lorna gave her a big hug, telling her it was so lovely to see her again. Audrey moved back to her chair. Sitting down, she patted the stool in front of her. "Come you two, sit! Tell me all about school and how you two found each other again and what brought you both home for the holiday?"

They both moved over to the stool and sat down. Phillip reached for Lorna's hand, raising it up to show his mother her ring. Audrey gasped, covering her mouth as tears filled her eyes again.

"Oh Phillip, I couldn't be happier. I knew someday you two would find your way back to each other. True love has a way of doing just that! Phillip, I got to know this beautiful girl here when she was staying us. You have yourself a wonderful girl. I'm so happy for the both of you. So how'd it all happen? How did you purpose and where? Lorna, please tell me that my son was a gentleman and got down on one knee?" Audrey let out a slight chuckle and leaned slowly back in her chair.

Phillip and Lorna looked at each other. Lorna took her hand, slid it into Phillip's, and their fingers tangled together. Lorna said with a shy tone, "Yes, Mrs. Powell, your son was a complete gentleman and very romantic." She gazed at Phillip with a whimsical smile on her face.

Phillip told his mother how he tricked Lorna into trying on rings in the jewelry store and without her knowing it she had picked out her own ring. He told her of the call he'd made for reservations at The Fisher Inn in Frankenmuth. He told of how he explained to the inn that he was going to ask the love of his life to marry him and that it had to be romantic with flowers and champagne, how he'd planned their weekend at Frankenmuth for right after midterms so they could relax and enjoy their time there.

Everything went as planned and Lorna had no idea, he told his mother, turning his head sideways to look at Lorna with a sheepish look on his face. Returning his focus to his mother, he told her that after they'd spent the whole day walking around from one store to the other, they went back to their room. He'd had the room prepared for their arrival again with champagne and red roses everywhere. He told his mother how he took his beautiful bride to be and got down on one knee holding the ring she'd picked out. He told her how much he loved her and that he couldn't imagine his life without her. That she was his life. Phillip then asked Lorna to marry him and she said "yes."

"Don't let him fool you, Mrs. Powell, it was way more romantic than that! He made me cry, it was so beautiful."

Audrey, very politely, said, "Lorna, please call me Audrey or Mother, whichever you feel comfortable saying. Mrs. Powell is so cold and formal and, Honey, you're almost family! To be perfectly honest with you, Lorna, I've always thought of you as part of the family. When you were here while you were pregnant we got to know each other quite well, and there is something so special about you that's so quiet and peaceful. It's so beautiful." Leaning forward and putting her hand on Lorna's knee, she told her, "I'm sorry that I just brought up when you were pregnant. I surely didn't intend on hurting you, either one of you."

"It's fine, Mrs...Audrey. I'm dealing with it, and every day gets a little better. Now that Phillip knows, I don't feel alone in this world of hurt by myself." Phillip squeezed her hand.

"Mother had I known about Lorna being pregnant with my baby, I certainly would've been here for her. Father lied to her, telling her that I knew and that didn't care, and that I was going skiing with some friends from school, which was a complete lie! I would've given anything to be home last Christmas. Most of all to be here when Lorna delivered our baby and to help her through the most painful, devastating tragedy that no mother should ever have to endure, much less endure it all alone, all because Father lied to her," Phillip said.

As his anger started to rise, a lump formed in his throat and his eyes started to sting as the tears welled. "Mother, do you have any idea how I felt when I found out that Lorna had been pregnant with my baby? My baby! And I missed all of it, Mother! I MISSED ALL OF IT! I wasn't here for any of it because of Father. How can one person be so hateful and filled with pure evil? I hate him for what he's done to all of us and for what he's done to me my whole life. Father is truly my nemesis, and it will be my magnum opus when I destroy him." Phillip rested his elbows on his knees, leaned forward and put his face in his hands, sobbing.

Audrey placed her hand on Phillip's head, running her fingers through his hair, telling him it was going to be ok. She said, "Phillip, darling, it pains me deeply to see you in this much pain. You have to let it go or it will consume you. Hate is an ugly thing and you're better than that. I raised you better than that. You're a good person, Son, and carrying around all of this anger isn't good for anyone. I do have a question, though, something I've wondered about for a while now."

Phillip lifted his head and looked at his mother. "What, Mother?" He tried blinking the tears from his eyes.

Audrey touched Phillip's face, wiped the tears away, then she said, "Since the day you left this house you never called or came home once. Why, Phillip?" she said softly

Phillip sat straight up. He looked over at Lorna, then back to his mother. He said with a downcast face, "Oh, Mother, there is so much you don't know." Just as he was about to tell his mother about how the doctor was keeping her medicated for no reason at all, per his father's request so he could have his way with Lois in the middle of the night, how he had signed a contract with his father to go to the University of Michigan and how Lorna signed an arrangement with him, about the hush money he'd given her on her 18th birthday and how they both had had to leave school because of his father, there was a knock at the door. Vera entered to announce that lunch was ready.

"We'll resume this conversation at a later time. Let's go eat and celebrate your engagement," Audrey said, patting Phillip on the leg.

They went downstairs, ate lunch, and enjoyed the loud conversation. They laughed a lot and listened to everyone talk about the two of them getting married, the wedding plans, the date, where it should be, the cake, who they should invite, all as Lorna and Phillip sat idle in the background taking it all in with big smiles on their faces. They both were thinking how great it was to be home with family despite the fact they both had to walk away from their dreams.

The Settlement

Chapter 11

The next morning Phillip and Lorna woke up late. Lorna looked at Phillip, who still had his eyes closed. She gently leaned in, kissing the end of his perfect nose. Phillip cracked one eye open halfway, smiled, and said, "Good morning beautiful." He turned onto his back asking what time it was.

Laying her hand on Phillip's chest, Lorna said, "I think about 10 o'clock, somewhere around there." .

Phillip stretched, yawned. "How about we just stay in bed all day today?" he asked her, putting his arm under Lorna's head and pulling her close.

"I don't think we'd get away with it. I think they're all too excited for us to be home."

"When do you want to go visit your folks?"

"Umm, I'm not sure. Not today. Let's do something with your family, then maybe I'll visit them tomorrow."

Phillip was a little taken back, bewildered at Lorna's response. Narrowing his eyes, "I thought you couldn't wait to get home to see your family?"

"I do want to see them, but I wasn't completely honest with you about something," she said, sliding her hand up and down his chest.

Phillip lifted his arm, turning on the bed. He sat up, looking sideways down at Lorna. He said, "What Lorna? What didn't you tell me?"

Lorna stood up and walked over to the chair next to the desk. She lifted her robe to put it on. Walking back over to Phillip, she looked him in the eyes and told him, "Honey, I didn't tell you this because I didn't want to hurt you more than you already were about me being pregnant. But the last time my dad heard your name, to him you were the guy that got his daughter pregnant then left and never came back. My dad doesn't know the whole story, nor does anyone in my family know that we're engaged. To be honest Phillip, I'm scared to tell them. My dad wanted to kill you and now I'm marrying you. I'm not too sure how he'll take that. And to add fuel to the fire, we were both thrown out of college. How am I going to tell them about marrying you without telling them the whole story of why I was thrown out of school? Oh, Phillip, there's so many lies and secrets that I'm just not ready to bring my family into yet."

Phillip reached out, taking Lorna's hand. "It's ok really, I truly understand. I appreciate you sparing my feelings. We'll see your folks when you're ready, then we'll sit down together and explain to them about what my father did and how he kept us apart." Pulling her hand close to his lips he kissed her fingers gently.

"Thank you, Phillip, for being so understanding. How'd I get so lucky to have you? I love you so much Phillip," Lorna told him, leaning down kissing his lips.

"I feel the same way Lorna, every time I look at you. I wonder all the time what I did that so good to deserve someone like you. You've made me the happiest guy in the world." Standing up, he slowly untied her robe, sliding it off her shoulders. Just as it hit the floor, there was a loud knock at the bedroom door and Lois on the other side yelling, "C'mon you two, get up! Get up! Get up!"

Phillip yelled to Lois, "Relax! We're up! We'll be down in a minute." Looking at Lorna, he started to laugh.

Lorna bent down, picked her robe up and put it back on. She whispered to Phillip, "We'll pick this back up later," a seductive look of lust in her eyes.

"It's a date!" Phillip responded eagerly.

They both emerged into the kitchen. Everyone looked so happy and in cheerful tones they all said,

"Good morning you two!" Phillip rubbed his stomach saying, "It smells amazing in here. What are you cooking?" He moved closer to the pans on the stove, trying to see inside, lifting lids. "Yummy, bacon!" Minnie swatted his hand when Phillip pulled a piece of bacon from the pan. "Damn, Sugar! Things with you never change!" Minnie laughed. Looking over at Lorna, she said, "Make a note of this. He's been like this his whole life. He can't ever wait until the food is on the table. He's like a little bird out here, eating before anyone else gets it." Lorna looked over at Phillip, laughed, and then said, "Duly noted!"

Minnie asked if they wanted anything to drink. "Juice, coffee, or milk?" They both said simultaneously, "coffee please" and looked at each other and laughed.

Then they heard from a distance, "I'll have tea, thank you," as Audrey walked into the room gracing them with her presence.

Phillip turned, "Mother! How nice of you to join us. We're almost ready to eat. Are you eating down here with us?" he asked, looking doe-eyed at his mother.

"Yes, I'll join you. Minnie, I don't want much, just some toast with strawberry jam if it's not to much trouble."

"Not at all, Mrs. Powell. I'll have that ready for you in just a few minutes." Minnie rushed over to the counter to whip up some toast for Audrey.

"Thank you, Minnie. I'll be in the dining room when it's ready."

They all followed Audrey and one by one they sat down. Just as they were about to eat, Phillip saw Lorna drop her head to pray. Phillip said, "Wait, before you eat I'd like to say a prayer." Everyone looked over at Phillip in shock.

Phillip held out both of his hands. His mother took one and Lorna took the other. Everyone else followed. Phillip dropped his head, closing his eyes. He said, "Dear Lord, thank you for this food we're about to eat. Bless it for us and let it give nourishment to our bodies. Lord, thank you for letting Lorna and I get back home safe to our families, even though I got a ticket, which I deserved. Lord, thank you for everyone at this table that I call my family. I've been truly blessed by you and thank you, Lord, for giving me Lorna, the love of my life. You're such a loving, gracious Father, and we love you. In Jesus Christ name, Amen!" He opened his eyes, lifting his head, and everyone was staring at him in disbelief.

Audrey patted his hand, "Nice Son, very nice."

"A ticket! How fast were you going?" Richard asked with quizzical eyes.

"Well, Richard, I don't think that's important," Phillip smirked, winking at Richard.

Lorna reached over touching Phillip's hand and whispered, "Thank you for praying. That was nice."

Phillip sat looking at Lorna, squeezing her hand. He tilted his head to lay it next to hers saying, "You don't ever have to thank me for praying. It's my pleasure to pray," he replied with a smile.

Lois tossed a piece of her biscuit across the table. As it tumbled onto the floor, she asked with a mouth full of biscuit, "Phillip, what are you and Lorna doing today?" She whirled her hand in the air.

"Well, honestly, we haven't made any plans. We thought we'd stay here and do something with all of you today."

"Cool," Vera said

Phillip spoke up, "You know what I'd like to do today? I'd like to put up the Christmas tree. And before you say it, I know that Thanksgiving is in a couple of days, but I really want the tree up so I can enjoy it since I didn't get to last year. Mother, is Lily coming home for Thanksgiving?"

"No, honey, but she'll be home for Christmas this year. She will, however, be sad to learn she missed you for Thanksgiving. Honestly, honey, no one thought you'd be coming this year either. How long are you and Lorna going to be home for?"

"Well, we're aren't sure at this point," he told her, looking downcast at the table as his mother stared at him. She knew her son wasn't telling the truth about something.

Richard, trying to break the tension in the air, said, "Well, Phillip, if you want a tree up, then let's put the tree up. I know of a place right down the road that just got all of their trees set up so we can go there in a little while and get one."

Phillip looked at Richard," Thanks. This is going to be so cool."
Lorna looked at Phillip smiling. She seen a side of him she'd never seen before. He was so cute, like a little kid.

After they ate, Richard and Phillip left to get a tree. Lorna stayed back at the house with everyone else. She was afraid to go with them for fear she might be seen by someone she knew, and she wasn't ready for her family to know she was home.

About an hour later, the guys came bursting through the front door with a huge Christmas tree. Phillip was so excited he could hardly speak. They pulled it into the living room, making a mess of pine needles all over the floor. Lorna watched Phillip and Richard get the tree in the stand and trim some of the branches, getting it ready to decorate. He was so full of life and Lorna was so grateful she got to witness that side of Phillip.

Richard and Phillip trekked upstairs to the attic to bring down the boxes of decorations. Box by box, they brought them all down.

Audrey was right in the mix of helping. She seemed so happy to have him home, and Phillip noticed that she almost looked like herself again.

Everyone started opening boxes, pulling out decorations. The room was a loud roar of laughter as they all started to put the ornaments on the tree.

Before they knew it, the tree was done, and it was beautiful. They turned on the lights, bringing wide smiles to everyone's face. The tree was done, except for the angel at the top.

Richard got the ladder. He held it steady while Phillip climbed to the top to place the angel on the tree and then climbed back down.

Richard started a fire in the fireplace, and Minnie made hot cocoa and popcorn. They sat in the living room laughing and talking, some of them staring off into the fire realizing how nice it was not to have Theodore in the house, how calm, relaxed and happy everyone was with his absence. They played Chutes and Ladders, Easy Money, then the game of Life. They played for so long no one realized it was dark outside until the game was over.

They cleaned up the mess and ate dinner. With her face pushed against the window, they heard Vera yell, "Hey, it's snowing outside!"

Lois said in passing, "C'mon everyone. Let's go outside and play in the snow!" She ran to get her coat from the closet.

Phillip, laughing, said, "Umm, what are we ten?" as he walked toward the closet.

Lorna said, "Sure let's go, it will be fun." She smiled as she reached for her coat.

Phillip, Lorna, Lois, and Vera all went outside. The snow was falling so gracefully. The girl's kept sticking their tongues out trying to catch snowflakes. They went out in the barn where it was a little warmer. Phillip stopped at the tractor and looked over at Lorna with a smirk on his face. Lorna returned the smirk, then Lois caught them staring at each other and pointed her finger at the two of them saying, "OHHHH! You two did it on the tractor!" She laughed and ran out of the barn.

Everyone followed her out, Lois stopping in front of Phillip. She threw her arms around him and she said, "Thank you for coming home. I've missed you so much. Without you here this place has been like a prison. Today is the most fun I've had since Lorna lived here and then she left us too." Looking over at Lorna, she threw her arms around her, telling her she missed her, too.

Vera walked over to Phillip and hugging him said, "This house isn't the same without you here. Now to have the both of you here together is so nice! I wish you didn't have to leave again." She backed up, wiping the tears from her face. It was very moving to Phillip because Vera didn't say much, but when she did it was usually something profound.

Phillip said, "Thanks girls. It feels great to be home. How long we'll be here I'm not sure, but you know we will have to leave again soon."

They both said, "We know." Lois took off running and went up on the back deck toward the door.

Phillip yelled, "Where're you going?"

"Back inside, you nerd! It's freezing out here." Vera followed her back into the house.

Phillip and Lorna stayed outside for a few more minutes. They stood in the middle of the yard kissing as the snowflakes fell on their faces. Then Lorna told Phillip she was freezing too. They went inside, back to the fireplace. Everyone started yawning and before long they decided it was time for bed. One by one they all disappeared. Phillip thanked Richard for helping him with the tree, telling him it was fun. Richard told him it was his pleasure, that his and Miss Lorna's presence brought life back to the house and that it was so nice to see Mrs. Powell downstairs and smiling. They said goodnight to each other and Phillip took Lorna by the hand, leading the way upstairs.

The Settlement

Chapter 12

Phillip and Lorna retired to the bedroom. Lorna was changing her clothes while Phillip snapped on the light on his desk. He opened the box on top of his desk. He pulled out a silver chain with his class ring dangling from it. He hooked his finger around it, twirling it in the light. He cleared his throat to get Lorna's attention. She looked over at him holding the necklace with nothing on but his boxer shorts. His bare body rippled in the light and Lorna stared at him as it made her insides hot and flushed.

Snapping out of the trance that his hard body had put her, and now playing dumb, Lorna said, "What's that?" She knew as soon as she saw it. She remembered looking at that very necklace last year while sitting at Phillip's desk.

Phillip said, "This is the necklace I was telling you about, the one I'd planned on giving you to wear while I was away at school. But it didn't happen like that," his voice and eyes trailing off in the distance.

Lorna walked over to Phillip standing by the desk. Reaching up, she removed the chain balanced on his middle finger. Lorna eyeballed that necklace like it was the first time she'd ever seen it. Looking up at Phillip, she said, "I would've been proud to wear it, too." She collapsed it into the palm of her other hand.

Phillip reached back into the box on the dresser and took out a little key. Walking around Lorna, he bent down and slid the key into the hole in the bottom drawer. He opened it slowly, lifting up magazines, a book of poetry, and then he pulled out his leather-bound journal. Phillip opened it and started flipping through the pages. He reached the page he was looking for and stopped. He handed the journal to Lorna, requesting her to read it.

Lorna looked at the book, then up at Phillip, "Are you sure you want to me to read more of this? The last time I read this it made me sick to my stomach."

"Yes, this is the letter I wrote for you. I want you to read it. Please!"

"Okay, if you're sure." Lorna pulled out the desk chair and sat down. She flipped the book open to the entry Phillip wanted her to read. Taking in a deep breath and then exhaling, she began to read the page titled, 'Letter to a Friend.' As she read it, the tears ran down her cheeks. When she finished, Lorna closed the journal and looked up at Phillip. "Oh my goodness, that was beautiful. You did write me that. I don't know what to say, other than I love you too!"

Phillip approached her from behind, reached over the top of her and picked up the necklace. He opened the clasp on the chain, lowered his hands to her neck and laid it across her chest. Lorna lifted her hair as Phillip closed the clasp. Lorna grabbed the ring with her fingers, adjusting it on her neck. She stood up and turned, facing Phillip. Standing on her tiptoes, she kissed him long and seductively. Phillip brought both hands up around Lorna's face, cradling her head in his hands, and tilted her head to kiss her long. He nibbled on her bottom lip. Their tongues explored each other's mouth, then Phillip kissed her up and down her neck.

Lorna flattened her feet back on the floor, thinking to herself that Phillip tasted scrumptious. His breath was sweet and the smell of his skin was musky and rugged; it was delightful.

Slowly, she pulled Phillips boxers off of his hips, letting them fall to the floor. She pulled the chair out, guiding Phillip to the chair while she lightly touched his bare chest. Running her fingers down his six-pack abs, she pushed him gently down into the chair. Phillip reached over to the desk and snapped off the light, looking up at Lorna's big, beautifully alluring eyes as they rested enticingly on his hard body. The cold winter moon made a perfect glow on Lorna as she stood in front of Phillip. She slowly started to unbutton her nightgown revealing the naked cleavage of her perky young breasts. She opened her lingerie and slid it off her shoulders provocatively, staring into his eyes and biting on her bottom lip, teasing and tormenting Phillip. Her nightgown slowly fell to the floor leaving Lorna in just her white panties. Phillip reached out to touch Lorna and tried to pull her into him. Lorna swatted his hand away, saying in a near seductive whisper, "No-No-No," while waving her finger up at him. She then hooked her fingers into the rim of her panties and slowly bent over, letting them slide down her legs and onto the floor. Phillip watched eagerly. Phillip told her to stand still for a minute so he could look at her. He took a deep breath, "Lorna, you're so beautiful. You have a perfect body. You're so sexy and captivating!" Lorna didn't say a word. She moved into Phillip, wrapping her hands around his face, kissing his lips tenderly and long. Lorna straddled Phillip, then kissed all over his face, with feather-light kisses across his eyes and gliding her teeth up and down his neck.

Phillip lifted his hands to put them on Lorna's bare body. She swatted them away again. Moving in close to Phillip, Lorna pressed her warm breast against his hard body. Gliding her breast back and forth across his chest, she rose, straddling over Phillip. Lifting her hands up, she began to run her fingers through his hair. She grabbed the back of his head and holding onto his hair she forcefully brought Phillip's head forward into her warm cleavage. Guiding him to her nipples, he opened his mouth. Using his tongue, he washed her erect nipples while nibbling gently on them. Lorna's body was aching for Phillip to touch it, but it would have to wait as she enjoyed teasing him.

Lorna backed up. She slowly kissed and nibbled on his ear, down his neck, his chest. Using her tongue she licked down his hot, aching body to his waiting girth. Parting his legs, Lorna knelt down on her knees between Phillips' legs, rubbing her hands up and down his inner thigh, just barely touching his girth. Leaning up, she lightly touched her tongue to his girth, then washed her tongue up and down his shaft. She engulfed him in her mouth, moving her tongue around the top. Phillip let out a groan of pleasure. Lorna lifted her eyes to see Phillip with his head tilted back, eyes closed and mouth open, with both of his hands gripping the sides of the chair. Lorna continued to tease Phillip until she knew he couldn't take it anymore. Slowly she pulled it out of her mouth, kissing all over his stomach.

Phillip reached to touch Lorna's cheek with the side of his hand. He caressed her face with his fingers, pulling in his direction for her to move up to him. Lorna slowly worked her way back up to Phillip. She straddled him, sitting down on his bare lap. Phillip sat straight in the chair. As his hands rubbed all over her body, Lorna let him touch her.

With his hand, he cupped her behind the ear and pulled her closer to kiss her long and hard. His left hand cupped her bare

breast and played with her nipple. Lorna's breath became labored as Phillip rubbed her aching body, waiting for him to touch her secret pleasure.

Phillip nibbled on her ear, laying seductive kisses up and down her neck and across her bare shoulder. He stood, holding Lorna as she wrapped her legs around his waist. He held her as he walked to the bed, still kissing her deeply as their tongues awaited what was next. Phillip walked over to the edge of the bed and slowly lowered Lorna down onto her back with her legs still wrapped around him. She released her legs as she felt herself fall to the bed. Phillip kissed her from stomach to breasts, licking her nipples and nibbling on them gently. Using his fingers, he lightly moved the hair from her face, kissing her neck and then moved back to her mouth. Phillip slid down her stomach and got to his knees in front of her this time. Lorna kept her legs on Phillip's shoulders as he slowly kissed her legs to her inner thighs. Moving to the middle of her legs, he took his tongue and licked lightly around in circles. Moving up and down, he washed Lorna with his tongue as she let out sounds of pleasure. Moving away from her, he kissed her stomach, traveled back down to her thighs, and again to her middle, teasing her as she teased him. Lorna lifted her head as she pushed Phillip off of her, telling him she wanted all of him. Phillip slowly moved his way back up to Lorna's lips as he reached down to guide himself inside her. Phillip stood,, placing his feet flat on the floor, and pulled Lorna closer to the edge of the bed. Holding onto her hips, he lifted Lorna's butt off the bed as he moved slowly, teasing Lorna this time. Phillip watched Lorna. Her head was tipped back, her eyes were closed, and she had both hands tightly wrapped in the sheets, squirming with pleasure.

Slowly, Phillip started to accelerate his rhythm. Phillip watched the pleasure he was giving her and it made it even better for him. Lorna began to get restless, moving her head back and forth, arching her back and gripping the bed. Moaning, letting out throaty sounds, Phillip knew she was getting close. He slowed down again, looking at Lorna, as her eyes flickered open and she lifted her head slightly off the bed. Phillip couldn't take it anymore either. He picked up the rhythm again, moving faster and faster. He heard Lorna cry, "Oooo Phillip," as she found her release. Phillip tilted his head back, closed his eyes, thrusting a couple more times before he exploded inside of Lorna.

Phillip slowly released Lorna's legs and moved to the side of the bed. He laid down next to her, wrapping his arms around her and kissing her gently. He said with a soft, breathy tone, "You're amazing and full of surprises. You sure know how to tease and be provocative," he chuckled.

Lorna laughed, snuggling in tight to Phillip. They lay there for a while, catching their breath and listening to the rhythm of each others heartbeat with the sound of the north wind howling outside his window.

They got up, put their nightclothes back on, and crawled under the blankets. Lorna snuggled in close to Phillip, laying her head down on his chest. Phillip wrapped his arm around her, pulling her in close to him. Lorna said, "Can I ask you a question?"

"Of course you can. What's on your mind?"

"Well...umm, I was wondering.... if you don't want to tell me, it's ok, but I was just curious. Umm...how many girls have you had in your room?" she asked him, lifting her head slightly to look at Phillip.

"That's what you wanted to ask me?" He laughed out loud then said, "No other girls have been in my bedroom except for the people that live in this house."

"Oh ok. It's ok, really, I was just curious," she told him, rubbing her hand on his chest.

They laid there for a few minutes in silence, then Phillip, a smirk on his face, said, "I lied, I did have a girl in my room."

"It's ok; you don't have to tell me."

"Oh no, you asked, so you deserve the truth. I completely forgot about Peggy."

"You even remember her name. How long did you see her?"

"Umm, well let's see. I was in third grade," he told her as his voice trailed off.

Lorna popped up laughing and looked at him. She started to tickle him. "Third grade…gee wiz. She must have left a good impression for you to remember her and her name."

"She did. She was my first crush. She lived next door, her family was our neighbor. We used to play together all the time. Her family didn't have a lot because her dad had been killed in the war and her mom was alone with four kids. My mother used to help take care of them all the time. One day they packed up and moved somewhere south and I never heard from her again. She was so cute. She had freckles and dark brown hair that she always wore in pigtails. The kids use to pick on her and they called her Piggy Peggy. It used to make me so mad, but the kids were bigger than me so there wasn't much I could do. We became really good friends and I secretly had a crush on her but I never told her. And yes, she was the only girl that ever came into my room." He let out a deep breath.

"Awe, that's cute. Peggy left and never knew you liked her." Lorna made her bottom lip roll down into a frown.

"Yep, broke my heart. I never loved again until you." He laid his hands over his heart and let out a chuckle.

"Awe, you poor thing!"
They snuggled up tight in each other's arms, closed their eyes, and then fell asleep.

The Settlement

Chapter 13

Lorna woke up startled from another dream she'd been haunted by for months now, in which she could hear her baby crying. She rolled over, lifting Phillip's arm off of her. She slid herself to the edge of the bed trying not to wake Phillip. Standing up slowly, slipping her feet into her house slippers, she grabbed her warm, pink fuzzy robe and slid it on. Looking over at Phillip lying peacefully on his side with his hand tucked under his head, he never budged. She glanced at the clock, noticing it was almost 5:30 a.m. She tiptoed over to the door and opened it very quietly. Making it out into the hall and quietly closing the door, she took a deep breath and headed for the stairs.

Lorna briskly moved downstairs to get a drink, trying not to wake anyone. Heading for the kitchen, she stopped at Theodore's study. Her heart started to pick up a faster rhythm as she moved closer to the double doors and stood there contemplating whether she should go in. She got sweaty and Lorna felt like she was having a panic attack. Taking a deep breath, she laid her shaky hands on the handles of the dark-mahogany double doors and walked inside. It was dark and smelled of Theodore's pipe tobacco. The feelings and thoughts that whipped through her were like a hurricane out of control and all at once it made her feel nauseous. Lorna indeed could feel the evil in that room. She felt like she'd just walked into the devil's den. She walked over and snapped on the lamp at his desk. Lorna sat down in his big, butter-soft maroon chair and lifted her hands to rub them across the top of Theodore's handmade desk. She sat there, looking across the desk to the chair on the other side. The very chair where she had been seated almost a year ago when she sold her soul to the devil and signed the arrangement with Theodore Powell.

Lorna started lifting papers, looking inside things, and smelling things when she noticed that his bottom drawer was slightly open. Taking her fingers, she slowly pulled the drawer open all the way. Laying right on top was a folder that was marked confidential. Pulling it out, she put it on the desk in front of her and took a deep breath as she opened it. Her heart almost stopped when she saw what was laying right on top. The billing statement from Schlanderer & Sons jewelry store for her engagement ring. Her mouth dropped open as her heart started to beat so fast she could feel it in her throat. Oh my goodness, she thought, Theodore knows about Phillip buying my ring. Laying the statement down, she saw Phillip's contract that they both had signed. She read it, not understanding most of it, but she did understand the part where it pertained to her, where Phillip agreed that he would never contact Lorna Collins again. Angrily tossing it aside, she saw the arrangement she'd made with Satan himself. Her blood started to boil after seeing that Theodore had added a clause that he'd paid Lorna Collins a one-time lump sum installment by way of a check for $100,000 to never contact Phillip Powell again. It stated that if this arrangement, therefore, were to be broken, it was pertinent that Lorna Collins understood that all $100,000 (with interest) would be paid back in full. Now furious, Lorna thought to herself, "You prick." Lorna placed the papers back into the folder and closed it. When she returned it to the drawer, she noticed a leather-bound ledger. Reaching into the drawer again, she lifted it out and laid it on the desk.

She opened the ledger and flipped through it month by month. Lorna couldn't believe the amount of money he was taking from all the small businesses in the town of Yale. She flipped to the present month of November and saw all the repeated names with the same amount of money written in the same spots. Then she noticed one that wasn't there before; Margaret Nolan, $5,000, on November 1st. Lorna said out loud, "What the hell…" She flipped back to October and there was Margaret Nolan again. She looked at September, then August, all the way back to May in the amount of $5,000 each time to her friend Maggie Nolan. Her whole body was shaking, her heart pounded with fear, and her mouth went dry. With her eyebrows pushed together she said, "What the hell is going on? Why would Theodore Powell be paying my friend Maggie $5,000 every month?" She flopped back in the chair as her head spun. Wanting some answers, she thought to herself, "I'm going to see Maggie today and find out the answer to this."

Lorna closed the book and neatly put everything back where she'd gotten it. She stood up, took one last look around Theodore's beautifully decorated study, and reached over to snap off the light. She closed both double doors and headed into the kitchen for a drink of water. Lorna walked across the kitchen to the sink. Standing in front of the sink, Lorna couldn't get Maggie off her mind or the fact that Theodore knew about her and Phillip's engagement.

Lorna thought she heard a noise and turned to see what it was. All of a sudden, a hand came up around her mouth, squeezing her face tight as her feet were lifted up to her tiptoes. Lorna could feel the full length of his body behind her. He was incredibly strong and smelled like whiskey and pipe tobacco. "Well, well, well...if it isn't Lorna fucking Collins in my house again. You're like a filthy fucking cockroach that I can't get rid of, and I know that where there is one there is more of you...and it's upstairs!" Theodore Powell growled through clenched teeth behind Lorna's ear.

Lorna was so scared her whole body started shaking. Her heart began to pound so hard and fast she thought it was going to jump out of her chest. She tried moving her body back and forth to get away from him, but his grip was too tight. She wanted to talk but she couldn't move her mouth. Lorna tried desperately to make loud noises from behind the tight grip on her mouth, but Theodore told her to shut her mouth or he was going to snap her neck. He lowered her to her feet and started to pull her across the kitchen floor, both of her slippers falling off as he pulled her toward the door. Theodore opened the back door, dragging Lorna outside. It was so cold outside that Lorna instantly began to shake. The cold north wind howled as Theodore pulled her down the steps and across the lightly snow covered grass into the barn.

Closing the door behind him with his foot, he drug Lorna to the back of the barn. It was breaking dawn and Lorna could see daylight peeking through the cracks in the barn. Theodore took Lorna over to the wall, slamming her whole body up against it. Her head rammed against a hook on the barn wall, making her instantly dizzy. She felt something warm running down the back of her head and she knew she was bleeding. He moved his hand down off her mouth to around her neck and Theodore stood staring into Lorna's panicked and fearful tear-soaked eyes.

Theodore was almost nose to nose with Lorna. His eyes were cold as steel and his voice took on an eerie tone as he said, "I knew when I allowed you to go to the University of Michigan you wouldn't stay away from Phillip. I was testing you and, needless to say, you failed. So, Lorna, what is it about a whore like you that my son can't stay away from? Maybe you're a great piece of ass. Perhaps I've been doing the wrong girl all along." He quickly started to undo his pants. Lorna heard his zipper moving down. Her heart was pounding so hard she could barely breathe, and the smell of whiskey and tobacco smoke was so overpowering it was making her sick.

Lorna started to pray in her head, "OH GOD, HELP ME!!! Let something happen to Mr. Powell so this doesn't happen. PLEASE, GOD, get me out of here!" She happened to see that she had blood on the collar of her pink robe but she didn't care. All she knew was that she had to get free from Theodore's grip.

Theodore removed himself from his pants and started to lift up Lorna's robe, her eye's big and full of fear. He leaned into Lorna then said, "You're nothing but a gold-digging whore and you don't deserve my son or my money. That's why I took your son from you. There was no way I was going to let you raise my grandson." Theodore started rubbing all over Lorna's body.

Lorna was feeling so dizzy and everything was starting to look dark and prickly in front of her. Her thoughts were weak as she struggled to say, "My son? I had a little girl and she died."

Theodore said, "Well, that's what I let you think. No, Lorna, you had a son and he's very much alive and healthy, but you'll never see him in this lifetime. You'll never find him." He slid his hands up to her breasts, cupping them.

Lorna could barely breathe. She couldn't believe what she was hearing. She knew her baby was still alive, she could feel it. Lorna said between gasps for air, "WHERE IS HE!!!"

Theodore moved his face closer to Lorna's ear. "Lorna. Lorna, you'd be surprised how close he really is and what people will do for money." He reached under her nightgown and around to her butt. He placed his hand on her, started to rub, then said, "One thing for sure you do have a nice firm body. Maybe that's what Phillip likes about you and why he'd spend my fucking money to put that engagement ring on your finger." He started to pull her panties down.

Lorna kept thinking, my son. My baby is alive! Phillip! Oh I have to get to Phillip. Who has my baby? Where is he? Lorna started to feel woozy, she couldn't think anymore, and Theodore was about to rape her. As realization hit her, she got a pit in her stomach as she remembered seeing Maggie Nolan in Theodore's ledger. Oh my gosh! Could it be? Does Maggie have my baby? Lorna thought, I have to fight for my son! She started to squirm, moving back and forth to get free from Theodore. He kept tightening his grip around her neck as he was squeezing the life from her tiny frame.

"Hold still or I'm going to squeeze your neck so hard I'm going to fucking kill you." Then with a condescending tone he said, "What a great service I'd being doing for the world." He moved his hand between her legs.

All at once, Lorna gained inner strength. She saw a hay hook hanging on the wall right next to her. She kept thrusting herself side to side and with her right hand she reached out and grabbed it off the nail it was hung on. It was cold and heavy. With all the strength left inside her, Lorna brought it back and with a forceful thump she hit Theodore in the head with it. He released his grip from around her neck and fell to the ground with Lorna falling on top of him. She laid there trying to catch her breath. She was scared, but she knew she had to get up. Get up! Get up Lorna, she kept telling herself. I have to fight for my baby! I have to get up! She opened her eyes and with great strength she managed to roll off Theodore's body as it laid lifeless on the ground. She managed to struggle to her feet. Disoriented, Lorna grabbed a hold of a beam in the barn to collect her composure. She moved to the barn doors. Opening them took all her will. She started heading toward the house and in a blood-curdling scream, she yelled, "PHILLIP HELP ME!"

She fell to the ground and laid there in snow so cold she couldn't feel her body any more. OH GOD HELP ME! she thought.

Then she heard a man yelling her name, then she heard it again as it got closer to her. "It's Phillip! He's come for me. Phillip, I'm right here, help me!" she cried in a near whisper.

All of a sudden she felt big, strong hands grab ahold of her, and a voice said, "Where the fuck do you think you're going to?" Theodore had her around her waist, lifting her off of the ground.

Lorna wriggled forcefully until she broke free from Theodore. She took off running toward the back of the property screaming for help. The sky was cloudy and grey with a fog so thick she could barely see where she was running to. Her feet were so numb she couldn't feel them under her. Lorna was so exhausted she had to keep stopping to catch her wind. She could smell burning leaves and hear dogs barking in the distance. Looking behind her, she saw a dark shadow of a big man moving closer to her. She took off running again, coming to the end of the property, now trapped with no way out. Lorna began to panic, thinking Oh my gosh, what now? There's nowhere else to go! She looked up at the grey sky and begged God to help her.

Just like that, Theodore was right on her again. He grabbed her by both wrists and squeezed tight. With winded breath, he shouted, "Now what BITCH? Where are you going to go now?" He let out an eerie chuckle. He swung Lorna around to throw her on the ground when suddenly someone came up behind Lorna and hit Theodore in the head. The board hit the ground and Theodore lost his balance, falling backward while still holding Lorna's wrist. He fell through a pile of snow-covered leaves with lathed boards that covered a blocked-off old well that went down 20 ft into the ground. Lorna felt someone grabbed her around the waist and hold her tight. Theodore released his hands from her wrist, staring Lorna in the eyes, knowing he was about to die. Lorna hit the ground on top of someone while crying uncontrollably and trying to collect her composure. She turned to see who it was and with great surprise she said, "Mrs. Powell!" Lorna laid her head down and lost consciousness.

When Lorna regained consciousness, she was in the hospital. Phillip was next to her bed holding her hand. She said in a whisper, "Phillip," as the tears started to form in her eyes.

Phillip lifted his head, realizing Lorna was awake. He stood up and leaned over the bed to kiss her on the forehead. "Oh my gosh, you scared me. I thought...," he said, as his voice trailed off and the tears started to run down his face. He looked back at Lorna, "I love you so much, Lorna. I was so scared," he told her, rubbing her hand.

It all came rushing back, what had happened. Again, her heart started to pound fast. "Phillip, your father, where is he?" she asked in a frightened voice.

"You don't ever have to worry about Father hurting you again. My father is dead Lorna."

"Oh gosh! Did I kill him?" she gasped, covering her mouth.

"No, you didn't. He fell into a blocked-off well. The fall killed him. He snapped his neck when he fell. You didn't do it."

"Your mother, is she ok?" pitifully Lorna asked.

"Mother is fine. A little rattled, but she'll be ok."

"Phillip, my head hurts." She lifted her hand up to the back of her head.

"I'm sure it does. You had to have 14 stitches put in the back of your head and you have a concussion the size of a baseball.

"Oh my gosh, really?" She looked at Phillip with wide eyes.

"Yes, you have to stay here overnight, then you can come home tomorrow."

Lorna laid there thinking about home....home! "Oh my gosh, Phillip, I have something to tell you," she said, trying to sit up in bed.

"Babe, you have to lay down and don't get excited," Phillip told her as he helped her lay back down.

"Phillip, our baby is ALIVE!" Lorna said with excitement.

Phillip wrinkled his forehead, his eyebrows pushing down, "Lorna, that's absurd! You've been through a lot today. You need to lay still and get some rest."

"Phillip, I'm not crazy! Your father told me that he took him and gave him to someone else because he didn't want me to raise his grandson and I know who has him."

"Lorna, listen to yourself. That sounds crazy. Our baby was a girl. Remember? She/He can't be alive. You hit your head pretty hard and you think you heard things, but you didn't. Our baby is gone Lorna. Can we please stop talking about this?" Philip said in an irritated tone.

"No, Phillip! No! I won't stop talking about it. I told you before that I could hear my baby crying and that I felt that my baby was still alive. I know it sounds crazy, but it's not. Your father told me he took him. Yes, it was a boy! He took him and gave him to someone and I figured out who. Last night when I got up to get a drink, I went downstairs and I went into your father's study. I started looking through his stuff. Your father had the receipt from the jewelry store where you got my engagement ring. Then I saw his ledger, so I started looking through it. I saw my friend Maggie Nolan's name in there. Your father was paying her $5,000 a month, but it didn't say why. I traced it all the way back to May when she started getting paid. Phillip, I had our baby in April! Your father also said something to me when we were in the barn. He said that I'd be surprised at what people would do for money. Maggie was always complaining that her husband couldn't keep a job and how broke they were all the time. Then it clicked. Maggie! Maggie has our baby!"

Phillip looked at Lorna, "Who the HELL is Maggie?" he said, throwing his hands in the air.

"My boss from A&W. When I worked there, she and I got to be terrific friends. I thought it was weird that she hasn't tried to get a hold of me since she came to the funeral. I tried calling her a couple of times from school and her kids always said she was busy, that she couldn't come to the phone. It's all starting to make sense to me now Phillip."

Phillip stood looking at Lorna and the sheer desperation on her face, wanting to believe this was true; however, Phillip wasn't entirely convinced that any of it was true. The best part of having his father out of the picture was he'd be able to investigate the whole story.

Just then two police officers walked into the room. Walking over to Lorna's bedside they introduced themselves to Phillip and Lorna. One police officer took out his little notepad and his pencil. Flipping it open, he looked down at Lorna and said, "Miss Collins, do you think you're up to giving us a statement of what happened today with Theodore Powell?"

Lorna cleared her throat and started to sit up to adjust the pillow behind her back. "Umm, do I have to do that right now?" she asked the officer, looking downcast.

"Well, we like to get the victim's statement right away while it's still fresh in your mind. We'll go as slow as you need, but we'd like to get this matter taken care of as soon as possible," he said as he looked down at Lorna.

Lorna took a deep breath, reaching for Phillip's hand. "Ok, I'll tell you now." Phillip sat down in the chair next to the bed and listened to the horrifying story of what his father had done to the woman he loves. How he almost raped her and then how he ended up falling into the well. Maybe, just maybe, my baby is alive, Phillip thought. This isn't anything I'd ever put past Father. It sure sounds like something he'd do. He hated Lorna and me and to take our baby from us was his ultimate 'fuck you' to us! The story is most definitely worth checking out. The officers concluded their business with Lorna and left. Phillip sat staring at Lorna and told her how sorry he was for what his father had done to her. Lorna's eyes filled with tears. As she rubbed Phillip's hand she said, "It's okay, it's over. Phillip, please find our baby, and it will all be ok!"

Phillip went home to shower and collect some things for Lorna before he headed back to the hospital. He stopped in the gift shop and bought her flowers and a cute stuffed bear. He went back to her room. When Phillip walked into the room, Lorna was sound asleep, safe and warm. His heart started to pound and a lump formed in the back of his throat at the thought of how close he came to losing her today. Phillip knew there was no other woman on the earth he'd rather spend the rest of his life with than Lorna. Phillip got comfortable and stayed with Lorna all night.

The Settlement

Chapter 14

The next day, Lorna was released from the hospital. Phillip asked if she wanted to go home to her parents' house or back with him to his house. She immediately declined her parents' house. He reminded her that they lived in a small town and the death of his father would travel fast. Phillip told Lorna that he wouldn't be surprised if the whole town of Yale wasn't in the streets celebrating right now. Lorna told Phillip she wasn't going home to her parents without her baby.

Phillip looked over at Lorna, putting his hand on hers, he said with a wry smile, "Let's find our baby boy!"

Lorna looked at Phillip then said, "Seriously? Does that mean you believe me?"

"Well, it's definitely something my father would do. I have some questions. Like if our baby is alive, then who did you bury? Why did the doctor say that it was a girl? And why your friend Maggie?"

"Those are good questions that I honestly don't have an answer to."

They pulled up in front of the house and there were police cars out front still investigating what happened. Lorna asked, "Where is your father's body? Did they get him out of the well yet?"

"Yes, they went down in the well yesterday and got him out. I would imagine he's at the funeral home now," Phillip said without any remorse.

"Phillip, I have a quick question about your mom."

"Sure, what's up?"

"Well, did she tell you anything about what happened?"

"Yes, she told me that by the time she got to you out in the yard, Father was holding on to your wrist. He tripped on something in the yard, falling backward, straight through the leaves and lathed boards on the ground, and then down into the well. She said if she hadn't been there at that time to grab you, you might have gone down that well with him. Why do you ask?" he questioned her with a quizzical face.

"No real reason. It just happened so fast that I was just wondering if your mom remembered anything different than I did."

"Did she? Or is it the same as you remember?"

"The same, yes, exactly as I remember" Looking downcast, Lorna knew that it wasn't. She remembered Mrs. Powell hitting Theodore on the head. He then fell backward and Mrs. Powell grabbed her around the waist. Lorna thought to herself, "I will never forget the look of terror in his eyes when he knew he was about to die." She also knew that she'd never tell another living soul about what Mrs. Powell did and that it would always be just their secret.

"Okay then, you ready to go in now?" He leaned over, kissing her softly on the lips.

"Yes, I'm absolutely sure. Let's go."

Phillip drove past the cop cars and through the gates straight to the back. He parked his car in the barn and then they both went inside. The house was a loud buzz of joyous laughter and Minnie singing in the kitchen. When they walked through the back door, everyone met them. They all hugged Lorna gingerly, asking if she was ok and if she needed anything. They all offered their sympathetic words and told her how sorry they were that they didn't hear her screaming for help.

Minnie grabbed Lorna. As she hugged her, teary eyed, she said, "Sugar, if something would've happened to you I never would've been able to live with that." She slid her hand to her face, quickly wiping her tears. It wasn't often Minnie showed emotion like that. Phillip knew that Minnie cared about Lorna.

Lorna assured her that she was ok. She told them that she was exhausted and needed to lay down. Phillip helped her upstairs and into her nightgown and Lorna curled into bed. He asked if there was anything he could get for her and she told him no, she just needed to rest. He leaned down to kiss her on the lips and walked out, closing the door behind him.

Just as Lorna went to close her eyes, she heard someone tapping on the door. It opened and Audrey walked into the bedroom. She walked over to the side of the bed. Standing there staring down at Lorna, she said, "How are you honey, are you ok?"

"I am now. Thank you for what you did out there for me. You saved my life."
Audrey took Lorna's hand in hers. "I had to dear," she said. "Teddy had hurt enough people and it had to stop. There was no way I was letting him hurt you. Lorna, I love you, and I'm so proud to say that you're going to be a part of my family. I've honestly never seen my Phillip this happy. He would've never recovered if something worse would've happened to you."

"Mrs. Powell, how'd you know that I was outside?"

"I was awake when you got up and went downstairs. I never heard you come back up. I was coming down to ask you if you wanted a cup of tea with me when I saw Teddy's overnight bag and briefcase sitting by his study, so I knew he was home. Then I saw your slippers on the kitchen floor and I heard you scream. I hurried as fast as I could to find some shoes. I couldn't find any, so I put your slippers on and grabbed Richard's old jacket on the hook by the back door. I ran outside and by the time I got down the stairs both of you were gone. I could hear you screaming way out back. I followed your screams and then I saw Teddy holding on to you. I knew what I had to do. I waited for him to get close to the boarded-up well and when he did...that's when I hit him. I've never been so scared in my life. I was more scared that I wasn't going to be strong enough to hold you when he fell. I just knew I had to end everyone's pain in this house."

Lorna pushed her eyebrows together, "What do you mean, everyone's?"

"Sweetie, Teddy, was a monster and someone had to stop him. I've known for a couple of months now what he was doing to Lois. It made me sick, but I wasn't strong enough to do anything about it. So for the last couple of weeks, when he'd come in to give me my medicine I would pretend I took it and then I'd flush it down the toilet. I kept getting better and stronger, and now I feel wonderful. I feel better than I've felt in many years, almost like myself again."

Lorna said, "Audrey, there are some things you need to know. Phillip and I need to sit down with you and tell you. But if you don't mind, I'm so tired from the pain medicine they have me on I can hardly keep my eyes open."

"Sure honey, you rest and don't worry about a thing. You're safe now." She leaned down and kissed Lorna on the top of her head.

Turning to walk out of the room, Lorna touched her hand, "Audrey, one more thing. The story you just told me about what happened outside with Theodore will never leave this room. I promise you with all my heart that it will always be just our secret. Phillip will never know the truth of what happened." Audrey squeezed Lorna's hand saying, "You indeed are a blessing. Now get some rest and we'll talk in a couple of hours."

Audrey went downstairs to find Phillip in Theodore's study rifling through all of his papers. Audrey walked in and looking at Phillip, she said, "Is there something you're looking for? Maybe I can help you find it?"

"No, I'm just….," his voice trailed off

"Phillip, I called Lily. She'll be home tomorrow for your father's funeral."

"Ok. It will be nice to see her again. "Ahhh here it is!" he said, holding up a piece of paper. "Holy shit! Lorna was right all this time. She told me and I didn't believe her. Uh-huh, here it is, WHAT THE FUCK...!" Phillip looked down, reading. "What the fuck...he put me as the father and Lorna as the mother but has her deceased."

"Phillip, what are you doing, and what is that paper?" Audrey walked closer to Phillip.

"This, Mother, is the birth certificate for your grandson. Mine and Lorna's baby that father said died. Our baby didn't die. He lied! He told Lorna it was a girl and that she died. It was a fucking boy and his name is Franklin James Powell, born April 1956. That's my son! THAT'S MY FUCKING SON!!!" he cried as he handed the birth certificate to his mother.

Audrey took the paper as she sat down in a chair. She gasped, putting her hand over her mouth, as her eyes filled with tears. She let go of the birth certificate, letting it drift down to the floor as she sat there in shock. Audrey looked up at Phillip with her mouth hanging open, looking like someone had punched her in the gut. She stood up, reaching for Phillip, and she wrapped her arms around him she said, "OH MY GOSH! Phillip, I...I don't even know what to say. I'm so sorry son. I honestly had no idea."

"I know, Mother. Lorna kept telling me she could hear the baby crying, that she truly believed he was alive. Well at the time, we all thought it was a girl. Mother, my son, is alive--I have to go. I have to find my boy!"

Just then they heard a loud scream from upstairs. Phillip's eyes got big and in a panic he turned and took off like a bat out of hell to get to Lorna. He raced up the stairs so fast he barely touched the stairs at all. Running down the hall into his room and flicking on the overhead light, he found Lorna sitting up in bed crying. Phillip rushed over to her and in a panicked voice he said, "Lorna, are you ok?" Sitting down on the side of the bed he reached over to hug her. "Lorna, your shaking! Are you sure you're ok?"

Lorna said, "Oh Phillip, your...father. I was running and he was chasing me. I watched him fall into the well," she cried hysterically in his arms.

"Lorna, shhh. It's okay. It was just a bad dream. My father will never hurt you again," he told her, kissing the side of her head.

Lorna knew that Phillip was only trying to make her feel better, which was kind of him. What Phillip didn't realize was that Theodore Powell might be dead and he would never physically be able to hurt her again, but the memory of him falling into the well would haunt her for the rest of her life and sometimes memories could hurt more than physical pain.

Phillip backed up from Lorna. "Guess what I found while you were sleeping?" he said with a look of anticipation.

"I don't know. Hopefully, it's good news because I sure could use some," she told him, lowering her head.

"Yes, I think you'll find this over the top happy news. I started digging through Father's stuff in his study and I found it Lorna! I found it. Our baby is alive! I found his birth certificate and his name is Franklin James Powell. Lorna! Our baby is alive!"

"Wh...WHAT? Are you serious? Where is he? Let me up! We have to go find him," she cried, moving Phillip so she could get out of bed.

"Hold on there missy! You're not going anywhere yet. Doctor's orders are that you're to get complete bed rest for the next couple of days. Lorna, you've been through a lot, and I will not let anything happen to you."

"Phillip, please let me up! We have to go find our baby!" she said with haste.

"Oh, we will. Just as soon as you are recovered and not a second sooner. So lay back down and I'll have Minnie whip you up something to eat." He moved Lorna's legs back under the covers, then propped her pillows up. Phillip told Lorna to stay put, he'd be right back. "Oh, Lily will be home tomorrow for the funeral," he told her as he turned to walk out the door.

Lorna took a deep breath and let it out slowly. She thought, "Oh geez, Lily. Well, now that ruined my appetite. Can't even imagine what she'll say to me knowing I'm the reason her precious father is dead. Lorna laid still on the bed thinking about her baby, what he looked like, how big he was now, and if he'd even know that she was his mother. Her eyes filled with tears as she thought he probably had teeth now and was crawling. He would be learning to say "mama" and "daddy" by now. She thought, "I've missed all of that…" She became angry, wondering how someone could be so cruel as to take someone's baby away from them. He let me think I buried my baby. I've grieved for months over her/him…him! Wow, I have a son named Franklin. Not the name I would've given, but it is a good, strong name. Then she heard a tap on the door and as she looked up she saw Lois in the doorway.

"Hi, come on in," Lorna said with a big smile.

Lois walked in and pulled the desk chair over to the side of the bed before she sat down. She sat with her head down for a minute then looked up at Lorna. Her eyes started to sting as the tears fell down her cheeks. "Lorna, I just wanted to come up here to thank you from the bottom of my heart for

what you did for me. I'm so sorry you had to go through what you did, and I'm so relieved that you're ok. I honestly thought it was a joke when I heard that Mr. Powell was dead. When I found out it was the truth, I burst into tears I was so happy, but also sad that you went through all of that."
Lois dropped her head down, weeping.

Lorna reached over to take Lois's hand in hers and said, "I'm fine now, and Lois, you're free. You never have to worry about Mr. Powell ever touching you again. You're free," she said, as the tears ran down Lorna's cheeks.

Lois looked up at her and with a wry smile said to Lorna, "Thank you! Thank you so much!"

A few moments later, Phillip came into the room carrying a tray of food. "Oh, I'm sorry. Am I interrupting?"

Lois stood up and said, "No, I was just leaving. She's all yours." She moved out of Phillip's way as he walked over and placed the tray on the bed. He turned around facing Lois and she put her arms around him. "I love you, Phillip. Thank you for everything!" Phillip pulled her closer to him, hugging her tight. "I love you, too, Lois. I'm so sorry for what my father was doing to you. I just wish I'd have known sooner, but now your nightmare is over," he told her as he let her go.

Lois said, "Yes it is, and it almost cost Lorna her life." Lois turned toward the door and left the room as Phillip turned back to focus his eyes on Lorna. He saw that she'd already found the birth certificate he'd laid on her tray. She smiled, then laughed out loud, then cried. Lorna said, "Phillip, your father put me as the mother, but I'm deceased."

"I know, but that's an easy fix at the courthouse. We'll take care of all that after we get Franklin back."

"Franklin. Umm, I wonder where he got that name? I like the name, of course. It's my dad's name, but it's so grown up. I like Frankie. How about you?"

"I don't know why Father named him that. Hell, I don't know why my father did half of the things he did. I do like Frankie though...yeah, I like it."

Lorna sat up examining her tray of food. There was vegetable soup with crackers, a homemade biscuit, with a piece of homemade apple pie and a glass of milk. Lorna laughed, looking at Phillip, "Holy Moses! This looks yummy, but did Minnie forget who she was feeding? This is a lot of food!"

Phillip laughed, told her to eat what she could, and to make sure she ate enough to keep her strength up. They sat in the room talking and laughing while Lorna ate her dinner. They spoke of their plan and how they were going to get Frankie back. Phillip told her his master plan and Lorna added her ideas. Soon they came up with a solid, concrete plan. They decided they weren't going to doing anything until after Father's funeral. Lorna got up and went downstairs and visited with everyone for a little while until time for her and Phillip to go to bed. It was a long, exhausting day and they both just needed to rest.

The Settlement

Chapter 15

The next morning, Lorna was awakened by the
sound of yelling downstairs. She looked over,
noticing that Phillip was already up. The voices
were muffled, so she could hardly understand what
was being said, but she just knew it was about her.
She kept hearing a girl mention her name. Lorna
laid still in bed trying to figure out who the girl was
and then it hit her. Uh-huh, that's Lily. As her the
voice came closer to the bedroom, Lorna's stomach
flipped. Lorna was getting nervous the closer Lily
got to her room.

Lorna heard a knock at the door and then it flung
open. Lily stood in the doorway, dressed as though
she'd step off of the runway. She was beautiful.
Lorna could smell her Chanel No. 5 from across the
room. Lily was wearing a dark blue and white
striped button-up dress, long white gloves on her
arms, and an adorable hat to match. Holding

herself with poise and confidence, she looked all business, and definitely not someone you'd want to reckon with--until she opened her mouth, which told a different story. Lily had no couth at all. Some would say that she had a mouth like a sailor.

Briskly, Lily makes her way to the side of the bed with Phillip right on her heels, offering his apologies for his sister's boldness. Lorna pulled herself up, adjusted the pillows behind her, and with wide eyes she watched Lilly clutch her gloves between her teeth., pulling them off one finger at a time while trying desperately not to get her bright red lipstick on her white gloves.

Lily, staring directly at Lorna, said, "What the fuck is going on? You and Philly get engaged, Father tried to kill you, and now he's dead. Damn, when I left this town it was stagnant, nothing ever happened here. I finally break out of here and all hell breaks loose. Hell, if I'd known this much excitement was going to happen, I would've stayed in this boring ass town. Why wasn't I notified about this engagement and when is this wedding going to happen?"

Phillip interrupted his sister saying, "Can we get through one thing at a time? We're burying our father today, and you want wedding details. What the hell is wrong with you?" he asked her, throwing his hands in the air with his eyebrows pushed together.

"Please, Philly, who are you trying to kid? You and I are both thrilled that that cold, quivering pile of shit is no longer with us. This whole house is excited. And, for what it's worth, the whole damn town of Yale is thrilled that Theodore Powell will be laid to rest today! Our father was controlling, merciless, and used his power to intimidate everyone he came in contact with. He controlled every single aspect of our lives. We're free now from that bastard! Everyone is free from him," Lily said with a scornful voice, throwing her hands on her hips.

"Nevertheless, show some respect for our father," Phillip said with disgust as he let out a big sigh. "I'm glad Father is dead. Yes, he's treated me like shit my whole life. He's tormented this whole town for years. He kept mother drugged for years unnecessarily, then raped Lois for God knows how long. He kidnapped our son and then he tried to kill the women I plan to marry and spend the rest of my life with. So am I happy he's gone? Damn right I am! I'd rather spit on his grave than go and show that I even cared, but he was our father and today, only today, we must show our respect," he told Lily as he looked down at the floor.

"Cool it, Philly! You're such a nerd and always so damn dramatic." Lily shifted her attention back to Lorna saying, "This is going to be swell. I'm finally going to have a sister. Now let me see that ring my brother put on your finger." Lily lifted up Lorna's hand and put her eyes on the ring. "Holy shit! Tha...that's huge! We need to go shopping. We need to update your wardrobe because wearing a ring of that magnitude you need to dress for it. Not saying what you wear isn't ok, but, let's face it, they'd be fine if you were going for the pioneer look like Laura Ingalls Wilder, but if you're going to be a part of the Powell family, you need new clothes. We'll get your hair, nails, and makeup done. Ohhh, we have so much work to do on you! You're definitely a work in process, but this will be fun," Lily said in a condescending tone.

Lorna laid there not saying a word, not knowing what to say. She was completely taken off guard by Lily's reaction to her father's death, then her saying that it was going to be swell to have a sister. Lorna was no fool. They both knew they didn't like each other from day one and now she wanted to be best friends. Lorna looked up at Phillip with quizzical eyes as Phillip just shrugged his shoulders, not knowing what to say.

Lilly turned to Phillip, then back to Lorna, "I've met a new fellow and he's great. His name is Roger.

We've been courting for a while now and things are getting serious." Clapping her hands together with a big smile on her face she said, "I think he might be the one. Wouldn't that be cool to have a double wedding? We could go dress shopping together and plan our weddings together! Oh, Lorna, this is going to be so much fun!" she said with much excitement in her voice.

Lorna had no idea how to even react to that statement. She looked over at Phillip, who looked like a truck just hit him. She returned her gaze to Lily and smiling cheerfully she said politely, "Su...sure that will be swell." She smiled wryly, laughing, and pretending to find it amusing.

Lily pursed her lips together saying, "I've imposed on your morning long enough. I'll be down talking with Mother. The funeral is at 11. We mustn't be late, so let's get this over with. Let's put the spawn of Satan in the ground where he belongs." She patted Lorna on the arm, smiling as she swiftly glided toward the door and disappeared, leaving the smell of her perfume behind.

Lorna took a deep breath, exhaled slowly, and said to Phillip, "WHAT THE HECK WAS THAT? Phillip, I'm not having a double wedding with your sister or anyone. And what's wrong with the way I look?" she said, haste in her voice while patting the blankets down around her.

Phillip walked over to sit on the edge of the bed. He took her hand in his, trailing his eyes up to Lorna's, and said, "Babe, c'mon, do you think I'd let that happen? The way my sister goes through gentlemen callers, I doubt he'll be around by next week. It's nice to see her excited about something though. I can guarantee she won't be honing in on our special day." He stood up and patted her on the top of her hand saying, "Now, we need to get ready for Father's funeral. I never asked you, how are you feeling today?"

Lorna looked up at Phillip. She tossed the covers off and replied, "I'm still sore, but better, that's for sure."

Phillip said, "If you're not up to going to my father's funeral we'd all understand." He stood watching Lorna get out of bed.

"No, I'm fine. Honestly, Phillip, as cold and callous as this may sound, I need to go. I need to know for sure that he's gone and won't ever hurt any of us again," she told him as tears filled her eyes.

Phillip walked over to meet Lorna in the center of the room. He gently put his arms around Lorna as she laid her head on his shoulder. They held each other while she wept. Phillip reassured Lorna that she was safe now, that neither his father or anyone else would ever hurt her again. Lorna pulled in closer to Phillip. Feeling the warmth of his body next to hers made her feel so safe in his arms. She slowly backed up and lightly kissed Phillip on the cheek. "I'm going to take a quick bath and get ready to go." Running her hands down his arms as their fingers connected, Phillip applied resistance, holding on tighter to Lorna's hands and forcing her to look up at him. He thought she was so beautiful and it pained him deeply that his father had made her so vulnerable.

He took his hand, cupped her face, stating, "Lorna, I love you and you're safe. You know that don't you?"

"Yes, Phillip, I do know. It's just going to take some time to get over this whole thing. I'll be ok. We'll be ok. I promise." She let go of his hands and moved to the bathroom, closing the door.

Phillip went to join everyone downstairs. They were all dressed in black and awaiting the funeral. Audrey walked over to Phillip and Lily and asked them to join her in the study. They followed their mother into the study. She politely asked them to close the doors behind them and have a seat. Phillip and Lily looked at each other as if to say, "What's this all about?"

Audrey sat in Theodore's chair behind the desk. She looked up at both of them and began. "Ok, I've asked you both in here because there are a few things we need to discuss. I realize that we have to get going soon, but I have to say a couple of things." Sitting straight in the chair, she leaned forward to rest her arms on the desk. "Phillip, you're now the head of this house, which means you're in control of all of this. You'll oversee your father's businesses. I do apologize, I know how much you wanted to become a doctor, but that isn't doable now. Having said that, I'd also like for you to give your father's eulogy today. I know your bitter, and with good reason, of course, but he was your father and this day belongs to him. Now, Lily, you'll remain in school until you graduate this spring. After graduation you'll receive a suitable amount of money to go do what you want to do for your future, but not until you've graduated from Wellesley College. Do I make myself clear to the both of you?" She rested her hands on the desk folding them together.

Lily was sitting half on the chair sideways with perfect posture, hands folded on her lap, looking like a real lady. With respect, she said, "Yes, Mother, I understand," as she shifted her eyes to Phillip.

Lily was an ass kisser. Her parents never knew what she was really like behind closed doors. Phillip played no games. He said it just the way it was and everyone loved him for his honesty. However, Phillip wasn't so compliant as his sister. He adjusted himself in his chair and cleared his throat saying, "Like hell I'll run Father's businesses and give up my dreams! Not happening, Mother. Also, I'd love to give the eulogy today...let me tell all of these people what a great upstanding father, husband, friend and businessman our father was. Now that would be a great big fat lie now, wouldn't it?" Phillip stood and started heading toward the door.

Audrey said, "Phillip, please come back and sit down. I didn't mean to upset you. Please sit," she instructed him, waving her hand in the direction of the chair.

"I'm sorry Mother, there's nothing left to talk about. I will not run the business, after the holiday's, I'll be returning to the University of Michigan to continue my education. End of story!"

"Phillip, this is a conversation best left for another day. We need to get going now as it's getting to be about that time. Let's go to that funeral home and give this family and your father respect," she told him as she pushed her chair out and stood.

Philip turned to look at the clock hanging on the wall of the funeral home. It was 10:30. The funeral home was all set up with chairs and flowers. People of all age groups were piling into the funeral home. Person after person, young and old, walked to the front to view the body. Phillip had noticed that no one had offered their condolences or said one good thing about his father… and no one was crying.

Ron, the funeral director, waved Phillip over to him. Phillip grew up with Ron. They had gone through school together and had drank a few beers together on different occasions. Ron's parents had owned the funeral home for as far back as Phillip could remember. He was a nice guy who ended up marrying his high school sweetheart.

Phillip walked over to him in the corner as Ron extended his hand. They shook and Phillip said, "Hey Ronny, whats up?"

"Hi Phillip. My condolences to you and your family. I know you and your father never had the best of relationships, but I am sorry for his passing. However, I was just wondering if anyone was going to give a eulogy for your father?"

"Yes, I'll be speaking today," he thought angrily. "You just let me know when I need to get up there...ok?"

"Sure, I'll let you know." Ron laid his hand on Phillip's shoulder as he passed by, offering his condolences once again.

Ron walked to the front of the room as everyone was starting to sit down. He looked around, noticing that there had never been so many people in that funeral home at once and they were still coming through the door. There was a line from the casket out into the hall of people from all over who had come to view the body.

Ron said, "Excuse me, everyone, if you'd like to get your seats we will proceed now." He looked over at Pastor Carl, nodding to let him know it was time to start.

Pastor Carl walked up to the podium and opened his Bible. He rested his hands on the podium and looked up at all the people sitting and standing in the room.

He cleared his throat then said, "We are here today to show our love and support for Theodore's very precious family. Not only have we sensed our own personal feelings of loss over Theodore Powell's passing, but our hearts have been drawn toward them and will continue to be with them.

Finally, we are here today to seek and to receive comfort. We would be less than honest if we said that our hearts do not ache over this situation. We are not too proud to acknowledge that we have come here today trusting that God will minister to our hearts and give us strength as we continue in our walk with Him.

It is our human nature to want to understand everything now, but TRUST requires that we lean and rely heavily on God even when things seem unclear."

Pastor Carl then read from Proverbs 3:5. Trust in the LORD with all thine heart; and lean not unto thine own understanding.

Ron walked up to the podium. "At this time, I'd like to have Theodore's son Phillip come up to the podium to give his eulogy. Phillip could you please come up here?"

Phillip stood up from the front row where he sat with Lorna, Lily, and his mother. He buttoned his jacket while walking up front. Ron shook his hand again and gave him a sympathetic smile, walking to the side and leaving room for Phillip.

Phillip looked up, took a quick scan of the place, then looked over at his father lying in his casket. Phillip looked down and when he lifted his eyes, his jaw tightened and a frown covered his face. He said, "Hello everyone. As I stand here, I see friends and relatives and some I've never met before. You have come to be here for me and my family and to say goodbye to my father, Theodore Powell.

I could stand here and tell you how I admire my father, but, well, let's be honest with ourselves. There is nothing nice to say about my father." Phillip quickly looked over at the Pastor who stood against the wall. "Pastor, I appreciate the nice gesture that you gave on behalf of my father. You obviously didn't know the Theodore Powell that I knew, or the man half of this room knew. Hell, maybe all of this room." He returned his attention back to everyone else as he watched their eyes get big and some women gasped and covered their mouths, including his mother.

Phillip took a deep breath, paused and exhaled slowly, and said, "I would've liked to have been able to stand up here like a typical son giving a heartfelt eulogy about my father. I'd like to tell you that my father and I were very close, that I could remember doing all kinds of things with him growing up. I'd like to say to you that he taught me so many things and he was the kind of man that I was so proud of that I wanted to grow up to be just like him. I'd like to tell you that my father was a warm, gentle soul. But nothing could be further from the truth. The one thing I am proud of is that I'm nothing like my father. I loathed my father. He was a horrible human being. He made everyone's life miserable, including his own family. I look around this room today, and I see so many people that have done business with my father, other's that in one way or another had to deal with the likes of that man, and just hearing his name out loud sets your teeth on edge, so my saying these things to you today should come as no surprise.

It's what I'd like to say today to everyone in this room. There's a new sheriff in town. My mother mentioned to me before coming here that I was now in control of my father's businesses. So hear this, I hereby declare the town of Yale, all businesses, personal and otherwise, are now debt free from anything you may have owed to my father. The slate is clean. Never look back. The black cloud that once hung over Yale will be lifted. As of today, things are going to change!" The whole room began buzzing, some women begin to cry, and everyone was hugging each other. Smiles returned to everyone's faces. Phillip stood up front with a wide smile on his face revealing his perfect charm. He looked down at his mother. She smiled back at him, nodding her head and giving him her approval. He looked over at Lorna. She was crying and smiling all at the same time. She mouthed, "I love you," and he winked back at her. Lily had the look of a blank canvas, just blinking rapidly. Phillip said, "Everyone? Hello? Excuse me, everyone, can I have your attention again for a quick moment?" Everyone stopped talking and turned their attention back to Phillip.

Phillip said, "I would like to invite everyone...and I do mean everyone..... to come to the Powell Estate for my father's wake. Let's bury this bastard and go celebrate!" Phillip stepped down from the podium and walked over to his father's casket. He looked down at him and said, "Now that's how you make lemonade!"

They all returned to the house. Car after car started lining the street until almost the entire town of Yale was at the Powell Estate. Minnie, Richard, and the girls had the curtains all open and the sunshine was blazing through the windows. The food smelled amazing and the house was full of people laughing. It was so lovely to see and hear laughter again. There had been so much doom and gloom in that house that it was about time things changed. Everyone kept walking up to Phillip to shake his hand and offer hugs, thanking him for what he'd done.

A couple of hours had passed, and one by one the people started to leave. They all thanked Audrey, some still offering their condolences. Then the house was empty again and back to reality. Phillip stood in the formal living room staring out the window. Lorna walked up behind him and wrapped her arms around him. She laid her cheek on his back. "You did a good thing today. I was so proud of you," she said, as she squeezed him tight.

Phillip turned around to face Lorna. He stared into her eyes saying, "I love you so much. I'm so glad you were with me today." He kissed her gently on the lips.

"I'm glad I was there for you, too. I love you too...but, if you don't mind, I'm exhausted and I need to lay down."

"Absolutely, you go ahead. I'll wake you in a couple of hours," he said, watching her walk out of the room. Phillip stood in the middle of the room looking around. He saw a picture on the fireplace mantle of him and his father. They'd gone camping when he was ten years old and it was one of the very few times he could recall having fun with his father. Walking over and removing it from the mantle, Phillip removed the back of the frame to take out the picture. He popped it out to find his father's handwriting on the back. "Out of all the wealth a man could possess, you're truly my treasure Phillip...I love you!" Phillip's eyes instantly filled with tears. He had to read it twice to make sure he'd read it right. He said under his breath, "Why didn't you ever tell me that to my face?" He took the picture and tucked it into his front shirt pocket, then he went into the kitchen to be with everyone just for the distraction.

Audrey walked over to Phillip and wrapped her arms around her son. She looked up at him and said, "I've never been so proud of you as I was today. That was a good thing you did for everyone today Phillip." She leaned in to kiss him on the cheek. "Also, I've put some thought into this as well. Go back to U of M and finish your education. Phillip, I can't and won't stand in your way of becoming a doctor. You're a remarkable young man and I'd be so proud to say that my son is a doctor. I'm still leaving you in control of the businesses, so do what you want with them. I want you to get your son back, marry that beautiful Lorna, become a doctor and be happy, Phillip. That's all I've ever wanted for you...is to be happy!"

"Thank you, Mother. You have no idea how much that means to hear you say that to me. I love you very much."

Lily spoke up saying, "Well, I think you should've talked to us before doing what you did. Do you have any idea how much of Daddy's money you just gave away today?" Looking down her nose at Phillip, she pursed her lips and lifted her wine glass to take a sip.

"Father's money. FATHER"S MONEY! It was never FATHER'S money! To begin with, he was stealing it from everyone. Don't you get it, Lily? We've lived the life of Riley because our father was a thief. He took everyone's money and treated them like shit...including ME! Moreover, isn't it funny that now that you're talking about Father's money, he all of a sudden became Daddy?"

"Screw you, Philly! So now what? Are we going to be... p...poor?"

"Only if you choose to be, you've been going to a fine college so hopefully you can put your education to use. I, on the other hand, will finish school and be the doctor I've dreamed of being my whole life. I will open my practice right here in the town of Yale. Honestly, Lily, I could care less about money. I only want to help people. And if I end up poor in the end, so be it. There are way more important things to worry about and care about than money. I've had amazing women tell me before that money is the root of all evil."

Audrey smiled while reaching up touching Phillip's cheek. She said, "Son, you're nothing like your father. I'm so proud of the man you've become."

Phillip reached up to place his hand on hers and smiled at his mother. "Thank you. That's the kindest thing I've heard all day," then he disappeared through the doorway to head upstairs to be with Lorna.

The Settlement

Chapter 16

Thanksgiving came and went and the house was filled with newly found laughter. Lily returned to school and Lorna went to her doctor's appointment, had her stitches removed, and got a clean bill of health. Although the outside might have been healed, she still woke in the middle of the night shaking, her heart racing, remembering the terrified look on Theodore Powell's face when he dropped down in the well and knowing the truth, it was no accident.

Phillip rolled over in bed tossing his arm down to the other side and realized Lorna wasn't in bed anymore. He lifted his head, looked around the room, and she was nowhere in sight. He laid there thinking about the chain of events that had occurred. Things had been so crazy for a few days that he hadn't had a moment alone to process anything that had happened. Phillip rolled over onto his back, folded both hands under his head, and stared up at the ceiling. The house was quiet and he could hear the north wind blow against the window, making it rattle.

Phillip laid there thinking about his father. It didn't seem like reality that his father was dead. He got nostalgic as he looked back on his life. He could hear his father saying, "Why can't you be more like your brother? You always have to be the pain in the ass, you're nothing but a mama's boy. You were nothing but a mistake, Phillip. We should've never had you. You will never amount to anything. You're nothing but trouble and always will be." As a lump formed in his throat, he could feel his eyes sting as he squeezed them shut and a tear rolled down the side of his face.

Phillip's whole life hurt. He only had a handful of good memories with his father. He rolled onto his side and reached toward the nightstand beside the bed. He pulled the picture of him and his father down. He rolled onto his back looking at the picture. He could remember clearly the day that picture was taken. They went camping up north to Traverse City. They went hiking, fishing, swimming, and had bonfires at night while his father told ghost stories. It was one of the nicest times he could ever remember with his father, but his brother James was still alive then. In his father's eyes, no one could measure up to his golden boy James, and when he was killed in the war his father became more controlling, overbearing, cold and callous. He had died right along with James the day he found out James was gone. Phillip flipped the picture over, rereading what his father had written on the back. He traced his handwriting with his index finger as another tear rolled down his face. He laid the picture down on his chest and thought about Lois, everything she'd been through, and his mother. He thought of himself and Lorna, what they'd been through because of him, how his beautiful Lorna almost died because of his father, and how he had stolen her baby and let her think it was dead. All these horrible thoughts became his reality. He threw the picture across the room and said out loud, "You bastard! You got exactly what you deserved!" Phillip sat up on the side of the bed to collect his composure as Lorna opened the door and walked in carrying a tray.

Lorna looked at Phillip with a wide smile saying, "Good! You're up. Let's go, let's go, let's go get our son!" she said with excitement in her voice as she set the tray down on the bed noticing that Phillip looked sad.

Phillip, with his head downcast, said in a low monotone voice, "Okay, let me get ready."

Lorna sat down beside him on the edge of the bed. Laying her hand on his leg and looking at Phillip with his head hung down so sad, she said, "Phillip, are you ok?"

Lifting his head, he said, "Yes, I guess. I was just thinking about all the rotten shit my father had done to everyone for such a long time." Looking at Lorna with tears in eyes, he reached up to wrap his arms around her, and hugging her, he said, "I am so sorry for what my father did to you."

"Phillip, it's ok really. I'm fine now, and things will be even better when we go get our son."

"I know you're right; I just feel so guilty for what he did to you," Phillip said in a quivering voice.

"There's no reason for you to feel guilty, you had nothing to do with what he did. I've not once ever thought any different of you. Phillip, don't let that eat you up like that! Your father ruined your life ….. until now. Please don't let him ruin the rest of your life from beyond the grave."

Phillip let out a sigh. "You're right. You're so right. This day is about our son and bringing him home...where he belongs. Let me get ready, and then we'll go get him," he smiled a wry smile. He stood up and heading to the shower, stopped to take his cup of coffee off the tray that Lorna had brought him.

Phillip and Lorna left the house, heading straight to the police department. They got out of the car and headed through the doors. Johnny Tucker, a friend of Phillip's from the country club, was coming out the doors at the same time. He was a nice guy and everyone called him "Tuck." He had joined the force about seven years ago and he took right after his old man.

Tuck looked up with a wide smile. He said, "Phillip! Hey man, how are you?" He extended his hand and as they shook, his smile fell and he said, "So sorry about your father. How's your mom doing?"

Phillip introduced Lorna to Tuck and they shook hands. Phillip said, "Mother is adjusting, but overall she's doing well. Thank you for asking. Hey Tuck, can we go somewhere private so we can talk?"

"Yes, absolutely. Follow me." Tuck turned and headed back into the police station. Lorna and Phillip were right on his heels and followed him down a narrow hallway to an office on the right, almost at the end of the hall. Tuck flicked the light switch and walked through the door as the lights flickered then came on. Tuck sat down in the chair behind his desk and rested his elbows on the surface. He looked at the two of them, then said, "Okay, how can I help you?" He was puzzled as to why Phillip Powell was sitting in his office.

Phillip reached into his jacket and pulled out an envelope. He laid it on the desk in front of Tuck saying, "open that," as he leaned back in his chair letting out a sigh.

Tuck looked down at the white envelope and lifted it up. He opened it, removing the contents, which held the birth certificate of their son, Franklin James Powell.

Tuck read the whole thing. He looked at Lorna, then Phillip, and stated, "What the hell is this?" With a quizzical look on his face, he leaned back in his chair.

Phillip said, "That's mine and Lorna's son that my father stole from us." Phillip told Tuck the whole story, starting from the beginning. As Tuck sat listening to Phillip talk, the tears rolled down Lorna's face. After Phillip was done, Tuck sat up in his chair, cleared his throat, and then said, "Who the fuck...excuse my language, Miss." He quickly looked at Lorna, then back to Phillip, and stated, "Who would do something so horrible and evil?"

"My father. My father, Tuck. Theodore Powell was pure evil and I'm not sorry he's gone. He got exactly what he deserved," Phillip said on an exhale.

Tuck stood up looking at Lorna and Phillip. "Well then, let's go get your son!" he told them, sliding his hands in his coat pocket. Phillip looked over at Lorna with a smile, then they both stood up. They followed Tuck down the hall and outside.

Tuck asked if they wanted to ride with him, and Phillip told him he'd follow behind him.

Tuck looked at Phillip, "We're going to Dr. Kendal's office first, right?"

"Yes, Tuck. Let's go get that piece of shit first," Phillip said, as he pulled his car keys out of his coat pocket.

Following the police car into the parking lot, they looked over at each other, smiling. Lorna was excited and nervous all at the same time and she had butterflies in her stomach. They got out of their car, meeting Tuck at the door. They followed him through the doors that read Dr. Eugene Kendal, M.D. There was an elderly couple sitting in the corner together, a mother with her two little boys playing on the floor, and newborn waiting to see the doctor. Tuck, Phillip, and Lorna walked up to the counter. As the receptionist was hanging up the phone, she looked at the police and Phillip Powell standing in front of her.

The receptionist, Jenny, said with a quizzical voice, "Hi officer and Mr. Powell. How can I help you?" Jenny was a beautiful young girl in her early twenties with soft, chocolate brown eyes and long black lashes, and dark brown hair that was pulled up in a ponytail. Her face held a pleasant smile.

Tuck, while looking down at her name tag, said, "Jenny, is Doctor Kendal here?"

"Yes, he's in with a patient right now. Is there something I can help you with?"

"No, this is a private matter," Tuck said, walking through the doors to go into the doctor's area with Phillip and Lorna again on his heels.

Jenny jumped to her feet saying with haste, "You can't go back there. The doctor is with a patient!"

Phillip turned. "Jenny, is it? This has nothing to do with you. Go back to your desk and answer the damn phone. It's ringing!"

Jenny stopped suddenly, dropped her head like a scolded dog, then said, "Yes, Mr. Powell." She returned to her desk, answering the phone.

Tuck turned to look at Phillip. "Damn! We need someone like you on the force. You ever think of being a police officer?"

Phillip said, "No, never. I'm in medical school now to become a doctor."

Tuck said, "Nice! Really nice. We're obviously going to need a new doctor in town because this piece of shit is all done as of right now."

Just at that moment, Lorna's heart broke as she reflected back on the conversation she overheard between Dr. Kendal and Theodore Powell when the doctor was trying to talk Mr. Powell out of over medicating Mrs. Powell. She was sure that the doctor was a decent man, he was just under the control of Theodore.

The side door opened as the doctor walked out in the hall. He stopped, looked at the police officer and Phillip and Lorna standing in the lobby.

"Oh shit!" the doctor said as he stared at Lorna.

Tuck said, "Doctor Kendal, I'd like to speak to you. Is there somewhere we can go a little more private?"

"Yes, of course. Follow me." He led them across the hall and down two doors into his office, which looked like a tornado had hit it. He quickly removed stuff from the two chairs that sat in his messy office. "Please have a seat, " he told them, as he stood next to his desk.

Tuck said, "Well, by your reaction when you saw us, you know exactly why we are here." Tuck pulled out the birth certificate and handed it to the doctor.

Lorna finally spoke, saying, "Where is my baby?" as her eyes filled with tears.

Phillip walked over to the doctor and grabbed him by his lab coat, forcefully pushing him into a bookshelf behind him when he said, "Where is our baby you fat, useless piece of shit?" Tuck quickly moved in on the situation, telling Phillip to let go of the doctor. Phillip released his grip from the doctor and Tuck told Phillip that he'd handle it.

The doctor regained his composure, then Tuck said, "What can you tell us about the baby that was born to Lorna Collins that you delivered back in April?"

The doctor cleared his throat, stating, "You have to understand. Mr. Powell said I had to do what he told me or he'd ruin my life as a doctor. Ok, here is what happened. When Mr. Powell found out you were pregnant, Lorna, with his son's baby, he said there was no way he was going to let you raise it or have anything to do with it. Mr. Powell called me in to care for you and the baby. When you went into labor, he had it all set up that I was to fake an emergency C-section, ensuring that I'd have to put you under and you wouldn't be awake when your baby came out and you wouldn't hear him cry. I put you under and delivered a healthy baby boy, and Theodore had it all arranged to have the baby taken to the lady he'd paid to raise your son. Her name was Margaret something. I never saw your baby again after that day. Lorna, Phillip, I'm so sorry for what happened. I tried everything to talk your father out of doing this unspeakable act. I, for one, am glad your father is gone, Phillip. Your father was a bully with money and pushed everyone around in this town. So, that's the story. If I have to spend time in jail, it will be worth it to be rid of this enormous amount of quilt I've carried about your baby. I honestly feel like I've been set free today. I'm so happy this is out in the open and you can go get your son now. Also, the woman that has your baby knows it's your baby Lorna."

Lorna stood listening to every word the doctor had to say with her hand over her mouth and tears running down her face. Phillip put his arms around Lorna and hugged her, telling her it was going to be ok and that they'd get their baby back.

Lorna said, "Doctor Kendal, can I ask you something?" Her voice cracked as she tried to talk.

"Yes, of course, you can."

"Doctor, who did I bury?"

"Nobody. There was no one in that little casket Lorna."

Lorna broke down crying so hard her shoulders were bobbing up and down. She looked at the doctor, then said "Do you have any idea how hard that was for me to bury my baby and grieve for all these months? I always knew in my heart that my baby was alive. I could feel it all the time. I thought I had a little girl and it turned out to be a boy, a boy that is alive." Lorna was crying so hard she had to sit down. Tuck reached over to the doctor's desk and grabbed a Kleenex for Lorna.

Tuck said, "Okay, you two, it's up to you. Do you want to press charges on the doctor?"

Phillip sat down beside Lorna in the other chair, reaching to take her hand. What do you want to do? I'll leave this all up to you. I will trust and support your decision no matter what."

Lorna sat quietly for a minute then she stood up and walked to the doctor. She stood staring at Dr. Kendal and said, "All the time you took care of me when I was pregnant I got to know you. I had also heard a conversation that you and Mr. Powell had in his study one day. You tried talking him out of overmedicating Mrs. Powell, and I heard him threaten you and your medical license. I know you're an honest man with good intentions. What you have done to me is not your fault by any means. So, to answer your question Tuck, No I don't want to press any charges at this time. Doctor Kendal, you're free from Theodore Powell's secret and the nightmare he's had all of us living in."

Doctor Kendal reached out and hugged Lorna tight, "Thank you, thank you so much Lorna," he said, and then he let her go.

Tuck, looking surprised, said, "Are you sure this is what you want Lorna?"

"Yes, it's time this town was released of the noose that's been around the neck of the town of Yale. I'm so sick of how everyone has lived for years because everyone's been so afraid of Theodore Powell. Well, he's gone now, and it's time everyone got back to living their lives."

Phillip walked to Lorna, wrapping his arm around her waist and kissed her cheek. Lorna looked at Phillip, then said, "Are you ok with my decision?"

He laid his head next to hers. "I am completely ok with it. I'm a lucky man to have such a kind women like you, Lorna."

Phillip looked toward the doctor. "Well, Doc, today is your lucky day. You wouldn't happen to know where this woman Margaret lives would you?"

Lorna spoke up, "It's ok honey, I know exactly where she lives!"

"Ok, then I guess our business is concluded here."

Tuck said, "Let's go get your baby!"

They walked out into the parking lot, and Tuck asked Lorna what Margaret Nolan's address was.

Lorna told him down left on Brown Road, fifth house on the right, a yellow house.

Tuck said, "Okay, I'll meet you both there," as he opened his patrol car door, flipped on the siren, and sped out of the parking lot.

Phillip and Lorna hopped in their car and raced behind Tuck, down Yale Road, and turning left Brown Road. They drove down the dirt road a little way before Tuck spotted the house on the right. He pulled in front of the house and turned off the siren. He got out and met Phillip and Lorna in the middle of the street.

Tuck looked at the two of them and said, "Let's do this. Let's bring your baby home!"

The Settlement

Chapter 17

Tucker walked up on the porch and rapped forcefully on the door. Lorna and Phillip stood behind him. The door opened as Tuck dropped his head down to a little girl about five years old with blond, curly hair and big, blue eyes and dimples in her cheeks.

In a soft little voice, she said, "Hi," then she released a tiny smile that revealed a missing bottom tooth.

Tuck bent down saying, "Hi honey, is your mommy home?"

The little girl stood there for a minute with her tiny hand on the doorknob and yelled in a big voice, "Mommy! There's a police guy here for you!"

Maggie came around the corner holding onto a crying baby, yelling at the little girl for waking the baby. Maggie stopped suddenly, looking at the police officer and Phillip and Lorna standing on her porch. Maggie made eye contact with Lorna, turned on her heel and headed toward the kitchen. Tucker grabbed the door handle, opened the door and hurried around the little girl, and headed toward the kitchen after Maggie.

Lorna yelled through the door, "THAT'S MY BABY!'

"STOP MARGRET!" Tucker yelled, as he right behind her at the back door.
Maggie turned around with the baby in her arms. Tucker said, "Hand me that baby right now!"

Maggie burst into tears crying, "He's mine! I've raised him since he was first born. Please don't take him from me, I love him!" she cried while looking down at the baby.

Tuck reached out and took the baby from her arms while she resisted, pulling the baby back. Tuck forcefully took the baby as Lorna ran up behind him. Tuck turned, looking Lorna in the eyes. With a very anxious smile, he placed Lorna's baby boy in her arms. Lorna fell to her knees holding her son in her arms. Lorna hugged and kissed his little face, telling him how much she loved him. Lorna cried so hard and kept thanking God Almighty for bringing her baby back to her. Phillip joined her on the kitchen floor and hugged Lorna and his son Frankie. Lorna pulled the baby away from her chest to see his face. She let out a gasp, "Oh my goodness Phillip, he looks just like

you. He's got your dark red hair and green eyes."
Phillip leaned down, kissing his son on the
forehead. He took ahold of his little hand and with
tears rolling down his face, spoke to his son. "Hi
there little guy! I'm your daddy and this is your
mommy, and we love you so much." The baby just
looked up at them, then smiled. He already had six
teeth, four on the top and two on the bottom.

Lorna handed the baby to Phillip as she stood up
and walked over to Maggie. She reached up and
slapped her right across the face saying in an angry
tone, "You were my friend! I looked up to you.
How could anyone do what you've done to Phillip
and me and be able to live with yourself? You and
Theodore Powell took my baby from me and let me
think my baby died!" Lorna had tears running
down her face as she looked over at Tuck. "Arrest
this bitch! I'm pressing charges against her." Lorna
stepped back and watched Tucker turn Maggie
around and put the handcuffs on her as he recited
her Miranda rights. Maggie's husband was sleeping
in the back bedroom and the kids were playing.
Tucker woke Maggie's husband and explained the
situation to him. Maggie's husband ran into the
kitchen to find his wife standing there in handcuffs.
Maggie looked over at him saying, "This is all your
fault. If I had a real man that could hold down a
job, I wouldn't be in this mess right now," she
cried.

He stood there gazing at her, shook his head, and said, "I'll see if I can come up with the bail." He left the kitchen and walked back toward the bedroom.

Tucker took Maggie out and put her in the back of the squad car. Phillip and Lorna followed behind him. When he walked back to Phillip and Lorna he said, "You two going to be ok now? I wish you both the best, and make sure I get an invite to that wedding you hear?" Tuck extended his arm and he and Phillip shook hands. Phillip thanked him for everything that he had done for them and reassured him that they were going to be great now. Tuck just smiled, telling him it was his pleasure. He hopped in the car and smiled at Lorna holding her baby.

Phillip looked over at Lorna. "Well, my love, are you ready to take our baby home?"

Lorna gave him a big smile as she raised the baby up, kissing him on the forehead. She wrapped him in a throw blanket she'd taken off Maggie's couch on her way out the door and said, "Phillip, can I ask you a favor please?"

"Sure, my darling, what is it?"

"Can we please go to my parents' house first? I haven't seen my family in so long and so much has happened. I'd really like to show them their grandson and let them know you and I are getting married."

"Yes, absolutely, whatever you want. I have an order of business to discuss with your father anyway." Lorna quickly shot Phillip a glance, pushing her eyebrows together as a shred of concern crossed her face.

They got in the car with their baby and headed to Lorna's parents house. They headed down Brown Road onto Yale Road again and turned onto Kilgore Road. Phillip drove slowly and as they approached Lorna's parents house, her stomach did somersaults. Taking a deep breath and exhaling slowly, Phillip looked over asking if she was ok.

Lorna said, "Yes. No. I don't know. I haven't seen my family in a while. The last time my father even heard your name he wanted to kill you. Phillip, so much has happened since I've seen or talked to them that I honestly don't know where to even begin. I also noticed that my parents weren't at your father's funeral." Putting her finger into little Frankie's hand, he gripped her hand. Phillip's eyes trailed down to the baby and he smiled looking up at Lorna.

Phillip said, "Yes, I noticed that your family wasn't at my father's funeral. Lorna, our son is so cute! I honestly can't believe that we have a son. OUR son, and he's right here with us. Lorna, I'm so sorry I doubted you when you told me that you knew he was still alive," he said as he laid his hand on hers.

Lorna said, "It's cool. Really, if someone would have said that to me I would've thought they were crazy too. We have him and each other and now we are a family." Turning her head sideways looking into Phillip's green eyes, a smile flickered across her lips. "Okay, let's do this. Let's get this over with."

Phillip pulled slowly into her parents' driveway, then turned off the engine. He pulled the key from the ignition and said, "Okay, here we are." The side door of the house opened and her brother came running out in his sock feet and no coat. All you could hear was her brother Jake yelling, "Lorna is home! Lorna is home!" He flew up to the passenger side door. He put his hands to the window, cupped his eyes, and pressed his face against the glass. His eyes immediately went right to the baby. Jake yelled in through the window, "Sissy...who's that?" Lorna slowly opened the car door, pushing her brother out of the way, and propped Frankie on her hip, wrapping the blanket around him.

Lorna said, "Hi Jake! This is your nephew Frankie." She bent down to hug her brother. Jake looked at Lorna and with his little face scrunched up asked, "What's a nephew?" Lorna said, "This is mine and Phillip's baby, and you are his uncle." She started walking toward the house.

Jake said, "Did you have another baby Lorna?" with his little mind in wonder.

Lorna said, "Come in the house silly and I'll explain everything. It's cold out here and you don't have on shoes or a coat. You're going to get sick."

Alice came to the door, propping it open with her foot. "Oh for heaven's sake! I thought Jake saw things until I looked outside. Hi sweetie! And who is this handsome little guy? Phillip, what is going on?" she asked as she held the door open and everyone filed into the house.

Lorna reached up, hugging her mom tight. "Hi, Mom. I've missed you so much," she said with an enthusiastic smile on her face. "Where's daddy?" Lorna inquired, looking around the house.

"He's upstairs. He'll be down in a minute." All of her brothers and sisters came running downstairs to see what was going on. They trumped into the kitchen yelling, "Lorna," throwing their arms around her and hugging her. Her sister Kitty came into the kitchen, threw her arms around Lorna, and asked, "Hi sis, how are you?" She looked down at the baby.

When Lorna heard her dad coming down the stairs, her stomach flipped. Frank walked into the kitchen. With a surprised look on his face, he immediately looked over at Phillip standing quietly in the corner.

He looked back to Lorna. "You better have a good reason for this. How could you bring him back into my house after what the hell he done to you?" he asked, as he looked down at the baby.

Phillip walked over to Lorna, put his arm around her waist, and said, "Sir...if you'd let us…"

Frank cut him off in mid-sentence saying, "Kid's get upstairs...NOW!" He walked up to Phillip, coming nose to nose with him. Phillip never moved a muscle. Frank stood staring into Phillip's eyes. "How dare you come back into my house after what you did to my little girl! You got her pregnant and never came back to take on the responsibility. You just left her without coming back or even calling her. Do you have any idea what she has gone through...DO YOU?" Frank screamed.

Phillip tried to speak, and Frank cut him off again saying, "You're a low down, dirty rotten Fuck and you don't deserve a beautiful girl like my daughter. Why my Lorna keeps going back to you is beyond me. What she does is her business, but this is my house and you're NOT WELCOME IN IT. GET OUT OF MY HOUSE...NOW! Frank's face was red and sweaty, his eyes were bulging, and his right fist was clenched tightly together.

Lorna turned around screaming at her dad. "STOP IT, DAD! STOP IT! It's not Phillip's fault, and you're scaring the baby." The baby started to wail.

Frank snapped out of it when he heard the baby crying. "And who's damn kid is this?" he asked as he released his fist and looked down at the baby.

Lorna said, "That's what we've been trying to tell you Dad. This is your grandson. Franklyn James Powell," Lorna told him smiling.

Frank stood there looking at Phillip, then Lorna, with his eyebrows pushed together. He brought his hand up, rubbing his chin. He looked down at the baby then up at Lorna as though he was calculating how long she'd been away. "What the hell are you talking about...my grandson?"

Alice chimed in saying, "Lorna what are you saying? How can this be honey, we all know what happened to your baby. I don't understand." Alice stood looking at Lorna with her hand over her mouth.

"Mom, Dad, please sit down so we can talk to you. So much has happened and I've been busting inside to tell you both." Lorna and Phillip walked over to the kitchen table and sat down. Lorna started talking while holding the baby on her lap and her mom and dad sat down. Lorna began from the beginning and told them the whole story. Phillip piped in here and there helping her make sense to all the craziness. When she was all done talking, her mother got up from the table and walked to Lorna. Lorna stood up with Frankie in her arms as her mother embraced them both sobbing.

"Lorna," her mother said with a quivering bottom lip and tear-soaked eyes.

"What, Mom?"

"I'm so sorry I didn't believe you when you said that you could hear your baby crying and that it didn't feel like your baby was gone."

"Mom, it's ok. No one believed me. Heck, I even thought I was crazy at times. Please don't be sorry. And don't be sad, either one of you. I'm ok now. Theodore Powell is gone and I don't ever have to worry about him hurting me or my family again."

Alice reached up to wipe the tears from Lorna's face, then looked over at Frankie and put her hands out to take him. "Hi there, handsome. I'm your grandma," she said. Frankie got excited and threw his arms up for Alice to hold him.

Alice took the baby in her arms, hugging and kissing his little face. "Lorna, I can see a little of you in him, but he favors Phillip more."

Phillip smiled and thanked her, then Lorna said, "We also have more news. We're getting married." Lorna lifted her left hand to reveal her engagement ring.

Alice said, "Oh, honey, that's beautiful!. It's so big. Congratulations to both of you!" Looking down at Frankie, she said, "Did you hear that? Mommy and Daddy are getting married!"

Frank never said a word the entire time. He just sat there listening. "Phillip, I owe you an apology," as he stood and started to walk to the other side of the table.

"No, Mr. Collins, that's really not necessary. I understand you were protecting your daughter. That's admirable and I respect you for that, which brings me to something else. Please, Mr. Collins, sit back down. I'd like to discuss something with you."

Frank sat back down. He rested his elbows on the table, intertwining his fingers, and rested his chin on his hands. "What is it, Phillip?" he said in a stern voice.

Phillip sat up straight in the chair and leaning forward, he cleared his throat. "I know why my father named our baby Franklyn. My father thought you were one of the most humble, honest guys he ever knew. He trusted you and your judgment. You're a smart man, Mr. Collins, and you've got what it takes to run the business. My father always knew he could count on you to lead the men out there to get the job done and done on time. After my father died, the family business was handed down to me to run. I don't want to run it. I never have. You know that I'm in medical school to become a doctor. Mr. Collins, what I'm asking you is ……. will you run the business for me? I will make you and your family wealthy and take care of you for the rest of your life. I don't want any part of the business, and you know those railroads like the back of your hand. The guys out there respect you, and in a crisis I know that I can count on you to do the right thing. I know that you are a hard worker and will always make the business look good." Phillip paused, then said, "So... do we have a deal?" Phillip leaned back in the chair with an arched eyebrow, waiting for Franks response.

Lorna looked over at Phillip in amazement. She'd never seen Phillip act in such a professional manner. All grown up and so handsome, she barely recognized him.

Alice burst into tears saying, "Frank. Oh, Frank, we'd have the money to fix this house up."

Phillip spoke up, telling her, "We're going to rip it down and build a brand new house for you. First, I'll bring in my people and draw up a blueprint of how'd you'd like your home designed. Then I'll get a crew together and in the spring we'll break ground. I had planned on doing that no matter what Mr. Collins' discussion was today." Phillip drummed his fingers twice on the table looking at Frank.

Frank sat there for a few minutes thinking about what Phillip had said. He put his hands down on the table and rose, pushing the chair back as he stood up. He walked to the back door and grabbed his coat off a hook. He told them he needed to smoke and think about all of this. He went out on the back porch and paced back in forth, smoking. Phillip got up, excused himself from the table, and went outside to talk to Frank.

Phillip walked out on the porch and immediately put his hands in his pockets when the north wind blew at his face and pushed him back. Phillip looked up at the grey-covered sky. He watched the snow started to float down and could almost hear it hit the ground. "Looks like we might have a white Christmas this year," he said, looking up at the sky.

Frank looked toward Phillip and said, "Look, kid, I know what you're trying to do. My family and I aren't charity cases and I don't take handouts. I appreciate your offer, but I can't accept it." He walked to the edge of the porch and flicked the ash off his cigarette.

Phillip said, "Mr. Collin's, it's not like that at all. I know you're a proud man and don't take handouts. Sir, this wouldn't be a handout. You'd work very hard for your money and earn every penny you'd get. It's just that I need someone to run the business and if you don't take the offer, well, then, you'll leave me with no other choice but to hire someone I don't know. Honestly, Mr. Collins, I don't have time to go through the hiring process. I have to be back to school in a couple of days and that takes time, time that I don't have. I'd much rather hire a man I already know, one that knows the business and one that I trust," he told Lorna's dad as he sniffled his nose.

"So, you'd be my boss then...right?" Frank inquired, arching his eyebrow at Phillip while taking a hit of his cigarette.

"Well, yes I would be...but we'd do most of our communicating through the phone since I'll be at the University of Michigan. You'd have to travel to board meetings and close deals, but you can take Mrs. Collins and most places you could take the kids. It will require more paperwork, but on the plus side, you'd be home a lot more. I'll set you up with a company car and Big George, the driver, will take you anywhere you want to go."

"I'm just not sure Phillip. It's a lot to take in all at once. Would you mind if I think about it for a couple of days then let you know?"

"Not at all, talk to your family about it and call me when you've made a decision."

"Okay, then. That's what I'll do. Oh, and Phillip, I do have to say, I do apologize for me misjudging you and assuming the worst from you. Phillip, I heard what you did for the town. That was very kind of you. You're nothing like your father at all.

Theodore never done me wrong, but he did a lot of bad shit to a lot of good folks in this town."

Thank you, Mr. Collins, and the town is going to change; I'll see to that. One more thing while we're out here, I never asked you for permission for your daughter's hand in marriage," Phillip said, looking Frank in the eyes.

"You're a gentleman, Phillip. Your mother raised you right." Frank extended his hand and shook Phillip's. "Yes, you have my blessing to marry my Lorna. You keep in mind if you ever hurt my daughter again...I will hurt you!" Frank said with a stern face.

"You don't ever have to worry about that Mr. Collins! I love your daughter with all my heart and I'll never hurt her on purpose," Phillip smiled wryly.

"Okay then let's go in before you freeze out here," Frank chuckled, tossing his cigarette butt onto the ground.

Returning inside the house, Frank took Frankie and held him up, talking to him, telling him stories. All the kids came back downstairs and played with the baby. They stayed for dinner. When Phillip looked outside and noticed his car covered with snow, it was starting to come down heavy, he told Lorna to say her goodbyes so they could get going before the roads got too bad.

They got ready to leave. Phillip went out to start the car and warm it up for Lorna and the baby before cleaning it off. Running back up to the house, he opened up the door to help Lorna and Frankie down the stairs.

They all stood in the open doorway waving goodbye. Phillip turned to Frank and said "Mr. Collins, I'll be expecting a call from you within the next couple of days. Keep in mind this is a time-sensitive matter, so I'd appreciate it if you didn't drag your feet too long." He threw his hand up to wave goodbye.

Lorna, standing in the middle of the driveway waving goodbye, yelled one last time, "Bye Mom and Dad! I love you." The snow quickly covered her and Frankie's heads. They all got in the car as Phillip slowly pulled onto the snow-covered road and went home.

The Settlement

Chapter 18

The roads were slippery and Phillip drove slowly, making his way home. He pulled around to the back of the house by the barn. Turning off the engine, Phillip looked over at Lorna, then down at Frankie, and smiled, revealing everything that Lorna loved about him. Phillip got out of the car, running around to the passenger's side. He opened the door, taking Frankie from Lorna's arms when she got out. Phillip carried the baby while Lorna held onto Phillip's arm and they made their way across the snow-covered yard up to the back door. Phillip opened the door, stomping his feet at the threshold to knock the snow off, while letting everyone know that they were home.

Minnie was walking into the kitchen and stopped to look at Frankie. While rushing over to take the baby from Phillip, she said, "Mmmm, child, if I didn't know any better I'd swear this was you,

Phillip. He looks just like you when you were his age." Minnie held him on her hip. As she started to talk to him, Frankie began to cry, twisting his body with arms outstretched looking for Lorna. Phillip reached out and took the baby from Minnie. With a soothing touch, Phillip brought Frankie up to his cheek. Phillip said in his ear very low and soft, "Shhh, its okay. Daddy has you now." Frankie immediately started to settle down. Phillip closed his eyes, pressing his face next to his son's as he bounced him up and down slowly and placed kisses on his little head.

Audrey walked into the kitchen asking what all the fuss was for. As her eyes lit up with delight, they went straight to Frankie. Audrey covered her mouth as she gasped, "Oh my goodness, Phillip, he looks just like you!" She immediately walked over to Frankie and put her hands out to take the baby. Frankie tucked himself into Phillip, not wanting to go to Audrey.

Minnie spoke up saying, "Well, I'm glad it wasn't just me that he didn't want to come to," as she chuckled

Lorna moved over to Phillip. Placing her hand on the baby, she looked up at Phillip and said, "We're home, Phillip."

Lois and Vera came rushing into the kitchen and upon seeing the baby; they ran right over to him squeaking, "Can we hold him?" Lois didn't wait for an answer and threw her hands out, reaching for Frankie. He smiled at her, revealing his two bottom teeth, and jumped into Lois's arms.

Minnie said, "I'll see if we can find something for him to wear until you can make it to the store to buy him some clothes. I know in one of those boxes out back are some cloth diapers. I'll have Richard go fetch them for you."

Lorna spoke up saying, "Thanks, Minnie. My mother changed him and gave us a few diapers and safety pins, and those plastic pant things."

Minnie said with a chuckle in her voice, "Baby, you're going to need more than a few diapers. Let me send Richard out back to see what he can find." They all went into the living room and sat down. Phillip and Lorna told the whole story of how they got Frankie.

Phillip donned a mechanical smile and said, "Mother, I need to speak to you about something vital."

Audrey looked at Phillip, noticing the uncertainty that flickered across his face, and she said, "Absolutely. Let's go into your father's study." They both got up, heading into Theodore's study. Phillip opened the doors. Just then, a feeling of his father blasted him in the face. He could hear his voice and smell his pipe tobacco. It was almost overwhelming. Audrey's eyes began to fill with tears and she began to weep as soon as she walked in. This time, she let Phillip sit behind the desk, reminding him that all of it was his now. Audrey reached over the desk and grabbed a Kleenex to wipe her eyes. She quickly apologized to Phillip for crying in front of him, dropping her head down.

"Mother, there's nothing wrong with showing your emotions. I know you loved father, as I'm sure you're mourning for him. Father always told me that it was a sign of weakness that real men don't cry. Well, you know what Mother? I cry. I've cried several times in my life and I think I'm doing ok. Please don't ever apologize for being normal, being human, because father was wrong," Phillip said, as he pulled the big chair out sitting down.

"Well, thank you, honey, but I'm supposed to be strong for you. I did love your father very much when we got married and started our family. Over time and the loss of James, it changed him into someone I never knew anymore. I cry for a memory I once had, one that died years ago. Teddy was such a wonderful man when I first met him. I fell head over heels for him. We had such big plans for the future….," her voice trailed off as she lifted her Kleenex up to her face wiping her tears.

Phillip sat in silence watching his mother cry. It was so unfamiliar to him. His family never showed emotions. A lump formed in his throat as his eyes

began to sting from the tears that were filling his
eyes. One tear slowly ran down his cheek, and his
heart broke for his mother. Despite the feelings he
had for his father, it was pretty clear that at one
time his mother truly loved him.

Phillip sniffed, wiping the tears from his face. He
sat up, resting his elbows on the desk. He cleared
his throat. "Ok then, I needed to clear something
with you. We were at Lorna's parents before
coming home. While we were there, I had a
conversation with Mr. Collins. Mother I've asked
him to help me run the business. I'm expecting a
call from him within a couple of days to let me
know if he's accepted my offer. I realize I
should've talked to you before making such a bold
move, but I have to be back at school in a couple of
days. I don't have time to go through an interview
process, plus we know Frank Collins and he knows
the business, and he's trustworthy. Plus, I also
thought that this is a family business, correct? Well,
as soon as Lorna and I get married, the Collins
family will be a part of our family. So what're your
thoughts?"

Audrey shifted in the chair while adjusting her
dress, then said, "I think that's a fabulous idea,
Phillip. I can't think of anyone else more deserving
of such a promotion than Frank Collins. I have
always liked that family. They're good, honest
people. Phillip, I couldn't be happier and proud of

you for your decision. Yes, absolutely bring Frank on and let's all help each other." She looked at her son with such pride and her heart felt full.

"Okay, we'll see what Mr. Collins has to say when he calls," Phillip looked his mother in the eyes while twining his fingers together. He put his hands on the desk, pushed himself out and up, walked around to the front of the desk and let his mother stand. He said, "Mother, I love you. I'm terribly sorry for your pain. I'm also sorry that I have to go back to school so quickly, but I'll be back for Christmas." He walked closer to her, wrapped his arms around her and hugged her tight.

Audrey, looking somber, said, "Don't you worry about me, son. I'll be just fine. I have a new grandson to fill my days now and a wedding to plan. However, the thing that fills my heart with sorrow is the strained relationship you and your father had. He wasn't always like that honey. I wish you'd known the man I once knew," she said, as she offered a pleasant smile. "Go back to school honey, fulfill your dream, and I'll be right here when you get home." She rose to her tiptoes and placed a kiss on her son's cheek, then quickly took her thumb and rubbed the red lipstick off of his face.

Phillip groped for words, not knowing what to say. "Thank you, Mom, but I just feel so bad for leaving you so soon." Phillip looked downcast as he spoke to her.

"Shhh, don't be silly. I'll be just fine. Honestly, I feel better now than I have in a long time. It will all be okay, I promise," she said, squeezing his hand. They returned to the living room to join everyone else.

Richard came bustling in the back door with his hands full. Phillip jumped to his feet and rushed out to see what he was doing. Making his way to the back door, Phillip saw Richard hauling in a crib that had been stored in the barn. He was also bringing in some boxes that contained clothes which belonged to him and James when they were little. Phillip helped him in with the stuff and hauled it into the living room. Audrey jumped up with such a look of nostalgia...touching the crib.

"Are you ok, Mrs. Powell?" Vera asked with such sincerity.

Minnie jumped to her feet and went to Audrey. "Mrs. Powell, you gonna be ok? Would you like for Richard to take it back outside?"

"No, really everyone, I'm ok. I was just thinking of when I was pregnant with Lily and Teddy and bought this crib. Life was so different then. He was different then. Richard, it's fine. I'm glad it was still out there. We can set it up in the room next to Phillip's so that way they can hear Frankie if he starts to cry."

"Very well then, Minnie and I will dust it off. We'll get it set up for Frankie to sleep in tonight. Oh, in one of those boxes I saw some cloth diapers and other things you might find useful."

Audrey and Phillip started to open the boxes, discovering all kinds of things that brought tears to Audrey's eyes and a smile to Phillip's face. They came across the diapers, changed Frankie, and put him in some nightclothes of Phillip's from when he was that young. The crib was set up and Phillip and Lorna took their already sleeping baby upstairs to lay him down in the crib. They both stood watching him sleep with their arms around each other. Phillip leaned in kissing Lorna on the side of her head as she quickly looked up, telling him, "I feel so blessed. I cannot believe that he is ours. We have a son, Phillip." She drew Phillip in closer to her, hugging him tightly.

The next morning, Phillip opened his eyes, noticing that the morning light was just starting to break through the window. He looked over at Lorna lying next to him. She looked so peaceful; she looked like an angel. He reached over and traced her face with his index finger. Lorna slowly opened her eyes and looked at Phillip.

Phillip smiled. "Good morning, beautiful," he said, while taking his fingers and moving her hair from her eyes, tucking it behind her ear.

Lorna stretched, letting out a yarn. "Morning, handsome." Moving over and curling into Phillip, Lorna said in a muffled tone, "Can we just stay here all day?" She tucked her hands under her face.

"My queen, we can do anything you'd like. But we have a little boy that's going to be waiting for his mommy to come and get him very soon," Phillip said with a loving tone.

"You're absolutely right about that." Lorna smiled, tucking herself in closer to Phillip. "I'm so excited for this next chapter of our lives, but I'm also very nervous. What if he doesn't like me and what if I don't get this right? Phillip, I don't know the first thing about being a mother," she said, letting out a big sigh.

Phillip kissed the side of her head and told her, "Honey, you have nothing to worry about. He's your son, our son, and he'll know that we are his parents and we love him." Underneath his kind, reassuring words, Phillip was terrified too.

Phillip lifted his arm and Lorna rolled into his bare chest. Phillip wrapped his arms around Lorna and hugged her tight. He kissed the side of her head again and this time Lorna looked up at Phillip, kissing him back. Phillip rolled onto his side with his head on the pillow. Lorna's head was resting on Phillip's arm and he slid his hand up around her face as his fingers went behind her ear. He moved in closer to her body. Lorna straightened her body, coiling her leg around Phillip's leg, moving closer. They felt the warmth and full length of their bodies that was so inviting.

Taking Lorna by her head, Phillip pulled her closer to his face, kissing her all over. Cascading kisses down her neck, he slid his hand down her body and covered her breast. Lorna sat up, moving her body back and forth while pulling on her nightgown. Lifting her arms, Phillip helped her out of it as her perky young breasts popped out. Tossing her night gown to the end of the bed, Phillip rolled onto his back and slid his hands under the blankets. He lifted his butt up and removed his boxers, tossing them to the floor. Turning back to Lorna, he started kissing her passionately while he caressed her naked body. He cupped her breast in his hand and licked her erect nipples. Lorna let out a soft moan.

Phillip kissed all over her breast and made his way down her stomach to her inner thighs. He cupped her in his hand and hooked his fingers in her panties, slowly moving them down her legs.

He rubbed all over her body, making his way to her inner thighs as Lorna parted her legs. Phillip licked gently. With her eyes closed, Lorna slid her arms up over her head holding onto the pillow, letting out throaty sounds. Moving her head side to side, she licked her bottom lip and arched her back. She moved her hips up and down. Phillip knew that Lorna was in full pleasure. Phillip thought that Lorna was so beautiful and seductive.

Phillip slowly moved up to her stomach, laying soft feather-like kisses across her tight firm body. Lorna moaned, lifting her head to gaze at Phillip as he made his way up to her firm perky breast. She couldn't help but notice a look of pure pleasure on his face, which made her insides leap to attention with desire. He slid his hands around her breasts, holding them in his hands. He gently licked her erect nipples as Lorna bucked with desire. Her inner body wanted Phillip. He slid up her neck, cascading kisses up and down, and moving to her mouth. He stared intently into Lorna's eyes. His expression was ardent, full of desire. He slowly nibbled on her bottom lip and then entered her mouth with his tongue. As their tongues explored each other's mouths, he slid his hands up her arms to join his hands with hers above her head on the pillow. As their fingers intertwined with each other, he lifted his body and entered her. He stared into Lorna's eyes and in a soft voice laced with desire said, "I love you, Lorna." As Lorna found it hard to speak, she quickly murmured back in a breathy tone, "I love you, too, Phillip." He kissed her long and deep.

Moving their hips in sync with each other, Phillip laid his head beside Lorna's as he picked up speed. Lorna cried, "Ahhh, Phillip," as the pressure was building inexorably inside of her. She couldn't control it anymore and she released her inner body and exploded inside.

Breathing heavily, Phillip moved faster, then released himself inside Lorna. He collapsed on top of her. They lay there catching their breath with their hearts beating in perfect rhythm. Phillip removed himself from Lorna and fell back on the bed. He laid there staring up at the ceiling with one hand on his bare chest. They looked at each other and smiled. At that moment, they heard Frankie start to cry. Lorna's eyes got big, as her mouth formed the shape of an O, and Phillip said, "Well, that was perfect timing" and chuckled.

They quickly jumped up and got dressed. They made their way to the baby's bedroom. Opening the door, there was Frankie sitting up in his crib. Lorna rushed to him and picked him up. "Shhh," she said, "everything's ok. Mommy has you!" She held him close to her, kissing his little head.

Phillip walked over to them and put his hand on his son. He reassured Frankie that he was ok. They changed his diaper and went downstairs to get breakfast. Minnie was in the kitchen already and making oatmeal. Everyone ate, then played with the baby. Phillip and Lorna left a couple of hours later to go shopping at JCPenney's in downtown Port Huron. They shopped for Frankie and when they returned hours later with half the store, Frankie had everything that he would need.

A few minutes after returning home, the phone rang. Minnie answered, "Powell residence, how may I help you?" Minnie paused while she listened and said, "Sure, hold on just a moment please!" She laid the receiver of the phone on the kitchen counter and walked into the living room.

Minnie said, "Excuse me, Phillip, Mr. Collins is on the phone." Phillip got to his feet and rushed into the kitchen. His eyes caught Lorna's as he exited the room. They knew in an instant they shared the same thought.

Phillip picked up the phone. "Hello, Mr. Collins, how are you doing today? I do hope you're calling to inform me that you've decided to accept my offer?" Phillip closed his eyes and with pounding heart waited for his answer.

"Yes, Phillip, I have. I've talked it over with Mrs. Collins and we've decided it's an opportunity of a lifetime. We'd both like to thank you for trusting me enough even to consider me for the position." Phillip's eyes sprung open as he let out a big sigh of relief. "Great! I'm so glad you've decided to join me. I'll have our attorney draw up the papers today and I'll bring them by tomorrow for you to sign. At that time, we can go over some things you're going to have to know. I'll go over all that tomorrow, say about 1 o'clock? Would that be suitable?"

"That's fine, but I'm a little confused. Phillip, what are the papers that I'd be signing?"

"Mr. Collins, I'm not giving you a new position, I'm making you my partner. You and I will run this business together. You and I will be family before long and it only seems right that you're made a partner with me. If that is still ok with you?"

"WHAT? HOLY SHIT, Phillip! Oops, excuse my language. You just caught me off guard. Phillip, I honestly don't know what even to say."

"Just say yes, and we'll get started right away!" Phillip let out a chuckle, "Mr. Collins, you don't ever have to apologize for being you. That's one of the things I admire the most about you!" There was an awkward moment of silence. Then Frank said, "Well okay, Phillip. Yes, thank you. Again!" Frank said with much gratitude in his voice.

"You're certainly welcome. You deserve it. Oh, one more thing. I'm sending my guys over to your house this afternoon so we can get started on the blueprint for your new house. I want to get that done so we can get the details taken care of and start breaking ground in the spring."

"Wow, thank you again, Phillip. You're truly a blessing to this family."

"No problem, and that goes both ways. You're doing me a huge favor too. Plus, I love your daughter with all my heart." Phillip smiled. "Okay, I'll see you tomorrow at one."

"Absolutely, see you then Phillip. Give my love to my daughter and grandson."

"I surely will. Talk to you tomorrow." Phillip hung up the phone, mumbling under his breath, "cool." He let out a big sigh and walked to living room to inform his mother and Lorna that Mr. Collins had accepted his offer. Lorna smiled involuntarily, knowing in her heart that her family would now be taken care of and her father would get the money he deserved. Phillip looked at his mother as a smiled flickered across her lips and she nodded her head in approval.

Phillip ran his hand across his chiseled chin and laughed out loud, revealing his perfect smile. He said, "If you ladies would excuse me, I have some phone calls to make." He turned, heading into his father's study, and shut the doors behind him. For the first time, he took on the role of being boss and head of the Powell business.

The Settlement

Chapter 19

The next day, as promised, Phillip was at the Collins' house promptly at 1 o'clock. This time he was dressed in a suit and tie and carrying a briefcase. He definitely looked all business. Lorna and Frankie accompanied him so everyone could see the baby again. Walking through the back door that led to the kitchen, the air was filled with the aroma of cinnamon and hot apples. Alice had an apple pie baking; the house smelled terrific. Alice was checking it when the door opened. She smiled wide saying, "Hi, come on in. I was just checking my pie. It's almost done. I sure hope you can stay for a piece." Alice walked over to Frankie and took him from Lorna's arms. "Hi precious, wanna come to see Grandma?" She lifted him up, placing kisses all over his face, and Frankie smiled.

Alice walked to the stairs and yelled to Frank, letting him know that the kids were there and that they'd brought the baby. Frank wasted no time coming down the stairs. He kissed his grandson and Lorna on the cheek, then walked right up to Phillip. He extended his hand, shook with Phillip, and thanked him again.

Alice said, "Yes, thank you, Phillip. Your generosity is way too much though. How will we ever repay you?"

"Don't be silly, Mrs. Collins. I didn't do any of this looking for anything in return. We're all family and that's what family does for each other. Although, I'd love a cup of coffee if you have one."

"Absolutely! I'll get that right away." Alice handed Frankie back to Lorna. She got Phillip and Frank a cup of coffee before she and Lorna went into the living room with the baby.

Phillip sat down at the table. Laying his briefcase down, he snapped the locks open. He reached inside and pulled out the papers for Frank to sign. Phillip put them on the table and went over each page with Frank. When he was finished, he handed Frank an ink pen, showing him where to sign.

Frank lifted up the pen, then looked at Phillip and said, "Are you absolutely sure I'm the one you want for this job?"

"Mr. Collins, other than wanting to marry your daughter, I've never been more sure about anything.

Yes, you're perfect for this job. I like you, Mr. Collins. You're loyal, honest, and I love the way you love and protect your family. Quite honestly, Mr. Collins, I can only pray that I become half the father that you are. Lorna was a lucky girl to grow up in a house with so much love." Phillip leaned back in the chair, knotting his fingers together, and resting them on his lap.

Frank blinked back the tears that were forming in his eyes. He cleared his throat and said, "I'm sorry, Phillip, that your childhood was so lousy and your father was so rueful and treated you the way he did. Thank you for such a nice compliment, but honestly, Phillip, I don't do anything different than the next guy. I just try to work hard to provide for my family, teach my children right from wrong, and always give God all the Glory and go to church on Sunday."

Phillip took in a deep breath while lifting his cup of coffee and exhaled, looking over at Frank. Frank put the pen to the paper and signed on all the lines that Phillip told him to. He laid the pen down on the paper and stood. Phillip stood with him. As Phillip put his hand out to shake Frank's hand, Frank grabbed Phillip's hand, pulled him in, and wrapped his arms around Phillip hugging him tightly. Frank let go and one hand on Phillip's shoulder. Phillip quickly, out of the corner of his eye, looked down at Franks' hand. Frank said, "I'm sure proud of you, son. You're a good man, Phillip. You're just like your mother, and she's a downright nice lady. You have such a bright future ahead of you. Don't let anyone ever take that from you. I just want to say I'll keep things going on this end, and you go back to school and get your medical degree and become that doctor you've always wanted to be. I'll always be here for you, Phillip, if you ever need anything, and I do mean anything. Oh, one more thing, quit being so formal with me. Please call me Frank or Dad, whichever you feel comfortable saying." Frank lowered his hand from Phillip's shoulder.

Phillip stood there studying Frank with appraising eyes. He groped for words to say, not knowing how to respond. His father never once in his whole life told him that he was proud of him. Frank's kind words filled Phillip with unfamiliar emotions. He thanked Frank, then said, "I know I can trust you to take care of business here at home. That concludes this part of the business, but I'll leave you with a bunch of useful information that you'll need to read and familiarize yourself with. Oh! One more thing, I almost forgot!" Phillip reached into the inside pocket of his jacket and pulled out a check. He handed it to Frank, saying, "This is for you and your family to get you started." Frank took the check from Phillip. Puzzled, he looked at the check. His mouth dropped open. He looked at Phillip and while handing the check back to him, he said, "I can't accept this check. I haven't done anything to earn this and it makes me very uncomfortable. To be truthful, I've never had a check with so many zeroes on it."

Phillip said, "Frank, don't be silly. That's a sign-on bonus. I told you that I'd take care of you and your family." Phillip pushed the check back to Frank. Now, I'd like to see the blueprints that were drawn up yesterday."

Frank said, "Wow, Phillip! Thank you so much. Let me get the blueprints for you." He left the room, returning within seconds carrying a tube in his hand. He opened the end and pulled out the blueprints. As he spread them across the table, Phillip stood over top of them analyzing the prints. He said, "No! No. This isn't what I wanted!"

Frank was taken back by Phillips reaction and said, "I'm sorry, what?"

"Could you please get Mrs. Collins in here at once?" Phillip said in a stern voice. Frank called Alice into the kitchen. She rushed into the kitchen saying, "Good thing you called. My pie is about to burn up!" Letting out a silly laugh, she said, "Sorry I'll be just a minute, then I'll be out of your way." Grabbing her potholders and opening the oven, Alice pulled out the pie, set it on the counter, and hovered over it. "Mmmm, that looks and smells scrumptious," she said, as she watched the top bubbling with the hot steaming juices seeping out of the pie crust.

"Mrs. Collins, when you've finished with your pie could you please join us over here?" Phillip said while looking down at the blueprints.

"Oh sure, Phillip." Alice set her potholders down and walked over to the table. "Okay, now what can I help you with?" Alice looked at Frank with confusion on her face.

Phillip said, "All right, now I'm looking at these blueprints. What was the point of doing this if you were going to build the same house as you have now?"

"I'm confused, Phillip. What did you want us to build?" Frank asked while running his fingers through his hair.

"Well, here's what I was thinking." He grabbed a pencil and said, "Ok. How about if we do this, this, and this. Let's knock out this wall and put this over here. Let's add this, and the kitchen should be like this so Mrs. Collins has plenty of room to bake all those delicious pies. Let's move the staircase over here. Let's put the master bedroom with a master bathroom down at this end and a nursery next to your room. Down on the other end, we'll put four other bedrooms with bathrooms in each room. Downstairs, let's add a study for you, Frank, so you can handle business in private. Then let's add a family room with a fireplace so you can gather with the family. Outside, let's build a great big barn right over here. That's what I was thinking. Please add anything else you'd like." After crossing off and adding to the blueprint, Phillip lifted his head only to see Frank and Alice staring at the design with their mouths open.

Frank said, "Phillip, we can't accept this. It's way too much and way too expensive." He shot Alice a quick glance.

"Frank is right, Phillip. You're way too kind, but we can't accept this." She lifted her hand up and placed it on Phillip's shoulder.

Phillip straightened, adjusted his tie, and told them, "Look, Mr. and Mrs. Collins, this isn't open for negotiations. The house is going to be started in the spring and I need to make sure you're happy with what is going to be built."

Alice said, "Phillip, honey, it's way too much. We don't have enough furniture to even fill a house that size."

"Oh yeah about that…" Phillip raised his hand to his jaw and rubbed his hand across his mouth. "I want you to pick just the things that mean something to you. I'll be furnishing your new house with all new furniture."

Alice gasped and covered her mouth. "Oh dear, Phillip!" she said, looking over at Frank. "I've always believed that God has His angels on this earth, but I don't think I've ever met one until we met you. Phillip, you have got to be one of the kindest souls I know. There are no words to tell you what a blessing you are to this family. Thank you, Phillip. Thank you so much." Alice reached up to wrap her arms around Phillip's neck and hugged him tight, placing a soft kiss on his cheek.

Phillip returned the hug and said, "Now, if you wouldn't mind, I'd love another cup of that good coffee and a piece of that apple pie. The smell is driving me crazy. It smells delicious," he told her, as he let out a chuckle.

Phillip and Lorna returned home. Phillip got ready to leave the next day to go back to the University of Michigan. Lorna cried on and off all afternoon. They spent a quiet dinner together with Frankie. They talked about what the future held for them, making plans and dreaming out loud. Then Phillip said, "Lorna, before I head out in the morning, I have to know something that's been on my mind." He stared at Lorna.

Lorna looked up with the expression of "oh shit, now what" and then she politely smiled, "What would that be my love?" Her heart began to pick up rhythm.

Phillip leaned his elbows on the table. He leaned forward to get closer to Lorna's face and said,

"When are you going to make me an honest man and marry me? We need to set the date right now, so when I leave I will know that we will be married soon," he said, as he revealed a soft smile showing his perfect teeth.

Lorna let out a nervous laugh. "Well, go get a calendar and we'll set that date now." She laid her hand on the side of his face. Frankie started to fuss and Lorna picked him up, cleaned him off, changed his clothes, and she and Phillip put him into his crib. They went back downstairs and sat together in the family room with the fire burning. They carefully picked the date to get married. They hugged and kissed each other with much excitement in their hearts. Audrey came downstairs and she looked over at the two of them. They were smiling as though they'd just won a new car.

Audrey stopped, then said, "What are you two so happy about?"

Phillip said, "Come here Mother. We have something to tell you." Phillip patted the cushion of the couch and Audrey sat down next to Phillip. She looked at the both of them and wondered what the good news was.

Phillip looked at Lorna and smiling, said to his mother, "Mother, Lorna and I have set the date to get married. We've decided June 9th of next summer. Oh, and Lorna, I would like to have Pastor Tim marry us in the church you grew up in."

Lorna was overwhelmed. She was so happy. "Oh Phillip, I've dreamed my whole life of getting married in that church. My mom and dad and Brother were all married in that church. My parents will be so happy!"

Audrey jumped to her feet with excitement. She rushed over to hug both of them. "Oh my, that's only six months away. Lorna, honey, we've got so many plans to make in such a short time." She turned and walked away, all the while talking out loud to herself.

They both sat on the floor in front of the fire wrapped in a blanket making wedding plans. They decided who was going to be the maid of honor, bridesmaids, best man, and groomsmen. They talked about food and whom they'd invite. Phillip told Lorna that he was having a big house built for them out by her folks. He said that he wanted a house full of kids and wanted to live in the country with a barn full of animals; cows, horses, chickens, and cats. He wanted to have two big dogs to guard the house when he wasn't home. Lorna was so happy and excited; her insides lit up like the Christmas tree that was sitting next to them.

The next morning came too quickly. Phillip got up early, took his shower, and got ready to leave. Lorna's heart broke. She didn't want him to leave.

They went downstairs and Minnie was already up with bacon frying and coffee brewing. They ate breakfast and Phillip decided to go before it started to snow. Richard had told them that a blizzard was coming and Phillip didn't want to be on the road when it began. They all walked him to the door, hugged him goodbye, and told him to be careful. Phillip took his son in his arms, telling him that Daddy would be back and to be good for his mommy. Minnie took the baby and let Lorna say goodbye to Phillip alone. Lorna started to cry and wrapped her arms around Phillip. They hugged and kissed goodbye. Phillip assured her that he'd be back for Christmas and that she'd be so busy with wedding plans and taking care of Frankie she wouldn't have time to miss him. Lorna told him that wasn't close to the truth, that she already missed him, and he wasn't even gone yet. Phillip went outside and loaded his stuff into the car. He ran back up to the door to embrace Lorna one last time.

He wiped the tears from her eyes and said, "I love you Lorna...the future Mrs. Powell. I'll be back before you know it. I'll call you every day, and you'll be fine here. Everyone will take care of you and help you with Frankie." He hugged her tight, kissing her softly on the lips.

Lorna said, "I love you, too. Please drive safe and call me when you get there." She let him go, watching him get into his car. He waved goodbye to Lorna and drove away. Lorna closed the door and sobbed into her hands. Minnie came and wrapped her arms around Lorna, telling her it would be ok and that he'd be fine. Lorna took Frankie from Minnie and went upstairs crying.

The Settlement

Chapter 20

Christmas came and went and the New Year was there and gone. Now 1957, the wedding plans were in full swing. Phillip called home every day. He and Lorna discussed wedding plans. Lorna tried to make Phillip feel a part of all the planning. Lorna was shopping almost every day with Audrey and getting everything they'd need for the wedding. They invited Alice along many times; Audrey made sure that Lorna's family was a big part of the wedding planning. Alice was front and center when Lorna went dress shopping. They helped her pick out the most beautiful gown. They went to the First Baptist Church and Pastor Tim agreed to marry them. Everything was coming together right on track. Audrey hired extra cooks to help Minnie with all the food and to help serve it. They found someone to do the wedding cake and a good photographer, Geoffrey Sanders. He was an old friend of Audrey's. She'd met him while in college and he now had a very successful photography business, specializing in weddings.

Lorna had to appear in court at 9 a.m. for the hearing on Maggie. Lorna's heart broke when she saw her, knowing that they were such good friends at one time and now they didn't speak. Now Maggie is probably going to go to jail, Lorna thought. She stood in front of the judge as he asked Lorna one more time if she wanted to press charges on Margaret. Lorna thought of all her blessings and what a wonderful life she had. She looked at Maggie, then to the judge.

With a shaky voice and tears forming in her eyes, Lorna said, "Your Honor, what's going to happen to her?"

The judge told her that Maggie would be brought up on kidnapping charges and she'd go to prison. Lorna's heart broke. She knew she couldn't do it. She was so angry at first, but now she had her son back and was about to marry the most incredible man alive. Poor Maggie, she thought, won't ever have anything if I send her to prison. "Your honor, I'd like to drop the charges against Margaret. I don't wish for anything to happen to her, just let her go home to her children."

The judge looked at her in shook saying, "Are you sure, Miss Collins?"

"Yes, your honor, I'm sure."

The judge looked over at Maggie and asked if she had anything to say. Maggie said, "Lorna, thank you so much. I'm so sorry for what I did to you and Phillip, and I'm sorry I ruined our friendship." Tears ran down her face.

The judge said, "Well today is your lucky day then. I'm dropping all charges. However, I'm not letting you off that easy. I'm putting you on probation for two years. What you conspired with Theodore Powell was wrong, and you deserve to be punished for your actions. Now, Mrs. Nolan, you're free to go."
He slammed his gavel down on top of the block of wood under it and just like that Maggie was free to leave.

Lorna took a deep breath and exhaled, knowing she'd done the right thing. Maggie walked over to Lorna and started to speak. Lorna put her hand up, cutting her off in mid-sentence. She said, "I'm letting you off the hook because of your children. They need their mother. Go home Maggie and forget you ever met me or knew me. I wish you all of God's blessings, but you and I are no longer friends!" Lorna walked away from Maggie with her heart broken.

When Lorna got back home, she walked into a house that was full and loud with laughter. Minnie came to the door and took Lorna's jacket. Lorna asked what was going on and Minnie told her to go into the family room and find out. Lorna did. As soon as everyone saw her, they jumped to there feet hugging her. Lorna said, "What's going on? Why is everyone here?" Audrey and Alice walked over to her and told her that it was her bridal shower.

Lorna was so overwhelmed she cried. She got everything she'd need to set up her new life with Phillip in the new house he was having built for them. They'd asked her how it went in court and Lorna told them what happened and what she'd done. Audrey walked over to Lorna and took Lorna's hand in hers. She said, "You make me so proud to say you're marrying my son. You're truly a beautiful person, Lorna. You're one of a kind." She turned to Alice and said, "You are a wonderful mother and so is your daughter. Alice, you have done a wonderful job raising this young lady!"
Alice said, "That goes both ways." We adore your Phillip and he's truly a blessing to our family as well. He definitely has your heart and kind soul. God knew what He was doing when He put our two children together." They both smiled at each other.

Phillip had asked his old high school buddies to be in his wedding. They met with Phillip when he came home on spring break and they all left for the store to get fitted for their tuxedos. Lorna and Phillip went ring shopping for his wedding band. They celebrated Frankie's first birthday, then Phillip was back at school only to return in time for his wedding.

Time was flying by so fast! The Collins' new house was underway, the foundation had been laid, and everything was right on schedule. Lorna's dress and her girls' dresses were altered and ready for pick up.

Phillip completed his second year of medical school. He pulled into the driveway two days before his wedding. The guys took him out for his bachelor party and Lorna's girls took her out. Lorna and Phillip finally met up with each other around 1 a.m. in the morning. Phillip was drunk and talking loud. Lorna helped him to bed and Phillip passed out. He woke the next day with a headache the size of New York. They had things to finish up and then separated for the night. Lorna went to her parents' house to stay the night and Minnie kept Frankie so Lorna could get ready for her wedding. Lorna's sister, Kitty, was very excited to have her sister there one last time with her. They stayed up half the night talking and laughing just like when they were kids.

Lorna was already awake when the sun started shining through the windows. She'd laid awake almost all night because she was so nervous and excited she couldn't sleep. Lorna laid there with her hand up and admired her beautiful engagement ring. She couldn't believe that at 2 o'clock she'd become Mrs. Lorna Powell. She heard a tap on her door. It opened and in walked her mother to say, "Lorna, honey, it's time to get up. You've got a big day ahead of you." Lorna stretched, throwing the blankets off.

Lorna went downstairs with her mom. Everyone was already up. As usual, her brother John was there. Lorna was so happy to see him. Everyone ate breakfast and began to get ready. Lorna took her shower, did her hair, put on her makeup, and they all left to go to the church. Lorna and the girls got dressed at the church and finished all the little things. It was now 1:45 p.m. and almost time for the wedding. People from all over were filling up the church. Phillip and his guys were all there and ready to go. Lorna was dressed in her gown and her mother was putting her veil on when her dad walked in the room. He stood looking at Lorna as a lump formed in his throat and he fought back tears.

Frank said, "Oh my, Lorna, you look like an angel. Phillip is a lucky man to get you. I'm so proud of you honey, and I'm so happy for you." He walked over to his daughter and hugged her, trying not to mess anything up.

"Thank you, Dad. I love you and Mom so much. Thank you for everything you've done for me and all your patience with me growing up," she said, laughing out loud.

"Lorna, that's what raising kids is all about. I wouldn't change anything about any of it."

Alice said, "Okay, you two, I'm going out now. It's almost time." Lorna's stomach flipped as soon as her mother said that.

Frank took his daughter by the arm and led the way to the doors. The bridesmaids were waiting for her and they all took their places. The music started to play, the doors opened, and one girl after the other walked down the aisle. The wedding march song began to play and everyone in the church stood up with all eyes on Lorna. Frank ambled down the aisle with his daughter hooked to his left arm. Lorna looked at Phillip standing there watching her walk to him. He looked so handsome, so grown up with his black tuxedo on. The closer she got to him she could see he was starting to cry.

Pastor Tim started by saying, "We are gathered here today to join these two in holy matrimony." He did all the talking and then Lorna and Phillip had to repeat after him as they exchange rings and vows in the sight of God, family, and friends. They lit a candle and kissed for the first time as husband and wife.

Pastor Tim said, "I'd like to introduce to you for the first time Mr. and Mrs. Phillip Powell." Phillip and Lorna had wide smiles on their faces and walked back down the aisle together. Everyone soon followed them out of the church. They walked outside, and everyone started to throw rice in their hair. Phillip had the company car and driver waiting to take them through town. The black car was all decked out with a sign in the back that read, "Just Married," and cans streaming from underneath. They drove through town honking the horn before they met everyone at the Powell Estate for the reception. They stayed until almost 9 o'clock and then the driver took them to the Metro Detroit Airport where Lorna and Phillip boarded an American Airlines plane and left for their honeymoon, a week in Hawaii.

When they returned home, it was back to reality and life was busy. Geoffrey Sanders had started courting Audrey Powell. The Collins house was completed. The new furniture had been delivered and they now lived in their beautiful new home. The old house was torn down.

Frank was doing a fantastic job of running the business just as Phillip had anticipated. Lily married Roger and now lived in San Monica, California. A town like Yale, Michigan was way to small for a girl like Lily.

Lorna, not wanting to leave her son, decided to continue her education at St. Clair County Community College. She enrolled in the nursing program to become a registered nurse and four years later graduated top of her class and received her nursing degree.

Phillip put six more years into U of M and graduated with honors, receiving his medical degree. Phillip had their new house built near her parents and they had four more children. They had an office established in town and Phillip opened his medical practice, just like he'd dreamed of his whole life. Lorna worked with him as his nurse. Her sister Kitty and Lois were hired by Phillip to be the receptionists. Doctor Kendal was asked by Phillip to join his practice and help him with his overflowing, busy office. Dr. Kendal graciously accepted and started right away, closing his office that was just about bankrupt. Vera stayed working for the Powell's alongside her Aunt Minnie.

Phillip had the First Baptist Church remodeled inside and out. He had a big cross placed on top of the church. Phillip and Lorna attended service every Sunday and were very active in the church.

Phillip was saved and Baptized and they dedicated all of their children to the Lord Jesus Christ. However, that didn't take away the guilt that ate at Lorna. After all those years, Lorna still woke in the middle of the night in a cold sweat, shaking, remembering how Theodore Powell died, the look in his eyes, and the secret she'd kept all those years.

ABOUT THE AUTHOR

Carolyn Alexander is a native of Port Huron, Michigan. She lives with Brian, her husband, and two cats Ricky and Lucy. She loves God and attends church on Sundays for worship.

<u>Beyond Redemption Trilogy</u>

1. The Whispering Bridges

2. Time in the Secret

3. Silk Prison Swords

Coming Soon!

Made in the USA
Middletown, DE
09 March 2019